RAZORBILL

## CREEPS

DARREN HYNES's first novel was *Flight*, published by Killick Press in 2010. Hynes has also appeared in theatres across Canada, including the Canadian Stage Company, the National Arts Centre, and the Stratford Festival. His film and television credits include *Lars and the Real Girl, Heartland, Republic of Doyle, Degrassi:The Next Generation,* and *Hockey: A People's History*. Hynes lives in Toronto. *Creeps* is his first novel for young adults.

ALSO BY DARREN HYNES

*Flight*

# CREEPS

## DARREN HYNES

razor
bill

RAZORBILL
an imprint of Penguin Canada

Published by the Penguin Group
Penguin Group (Canada), 90 Eglinton Avenue East, Suite 700, Toronto, Ontario, Canada M4P 2Y3

Penguin Group (USA) Inc., 375 Hudson Street, New York, New York 10014, U.S.A.
Penguin Books Ltd, 80 Strand, London WC2R 0RL, England
Penguin Ireland, 25 St Stephen's Green, Dublin 2, Ireland (a division of Penguin Books Ltd)
Penguin Group (Australia), 707 Collins Street, Melbourne, Victoria 3008, Australia
(a division of Pearson Australia Group Pty Ltd)
Penguin Books India Pvt Ltd, 11 Community Centre, Panchsheel Park, New Delhi – 110 017, India
Penguin Group (NZ), 67 Apollo Drive, Rosedale, Auckland 0632, New Zealand
(a division of Pearson New Zealand Ltd)
Penguin Books (South Africa) (Pty) Ltd, 24 Sturdee Avenue, Rosebank,
Johannesburg 2196, South Africa

Penguin Books Ltd, Registered Offices: 80 Strand, London WC2R 0RL, England

First published 2013

1 2 3 4 5 6 7 8 9 10 (WEB)

LIBRARY AND ARCHIVES CANADA CATALOGUING IN PUBLICATION

Hynes, Darren, 1972–, author
Creeps / Darren Hynes.

ISBN 978-0-14-318714-1 (pbk.)

I. Title.

PS8615.Y53C74 2013          jC813'.6          C2013-903338-6

Visit the Penguin Canada website at **www.penguin.ca**

Special and corporate bulk purchase rates available; please see
**www.penguin.ca/corporatesales** or call 1-800-810-3104, ext. 2477.

ALWAYS LEARNING                                        PEARSON

FOR LIAM

# JANUARY

## Unanswered Prayers

# ONE

Dear God or whoever,

　Could you make me popular so someone will see me and smile and the volleyball team would high-five me in the corridor and the principal might even say my name over the PA system? Could you make me strong enough to lift a medicine ball and do the flexed-arm hang and complete at least twenty push-ups so they won't call me faggot? Could you make me taller? It would be great not needing a chair every time I wanted something in the cupboard above the stove.

　Mostly though I'd just like you to keep Mom away from the train and Dad away from the Bacardi Dark and my sister Wanda away from Nickelback. Also her Diet Coke habit is out of control. Is it true that ~~aspirtame~~ aspartame causes cancer?

　This is a big one, God or whoever, but if you could make high school pass as quickly as possible I'd really appreciate it. I know I shouldn't wish my time away but it's hard to be somewhere when you don't fit in. Mom says that it's selfish because there are people who'd kill for another MINUTE let alone an entire three years. You'll wish for the time back, she says, but I doubt that.

I walked behind that girl with the dead father this morning. She didn't look back although I'm sure she knew I was there. Wearing sneakers and here it is January. No hat or mittens. Jacket too smal l. Marjorie's her name but Maple Leaf's what they call her. They say she's easy and loves it all the time.

Yesterday I humped the snow and had to pretend like it was a girl but then Bobby laughed and said: a boy more like it.

Your friend who humps the snow,
Wayne Pumphrey

# TWO

Something explodes against Wayne Pumphrey's back. He turns around just as a snowball whizzes by his chin. One hits him in the stomach. Another strikes his shoulder. They're the hard and heavy kind, the after-a-wet-snow kind. One comes awfully close to his eye. He raises his arms. "I surrender."

Four figures approach: Pete "The Meat" Avery, followed by Kenny Saunders, Harvey Stool, and Bobby Power. Pete is called The Meat because he lives in the weight room and has fat veins running along his biceps and can make his chest muscles move without touching them.

Bobby's grinning and Harvey's smacking his fist into his palm while Kenny rounds a fresh snowball.

Pete goes right up to Wayne and stops, then signals for the others to stop too. He smooths his almost-a-moustache and says, "Where do you think you're going, Pumphrey?"

Wayne goes to lower his arms but Pete makes a fist so Wayne keeps his fingertips pointed skyward and says, "Same place as you."

Pete takes a step closer. "Not ahead of us, you don't."

Wayne smells StarKist tuna on The Meat's breath.

Bobby folds his arms across his chest. "You always walk at the *back,* Pumphrey."

"That's right," Pete agrees. "Your place is behind us, Pumphrey."

"Not *too* close behind though, eh, Pete?" Bobby adds.

Pete nods and says, "That's right. Lord only knows what this pervert might try."

Bobby laughs. "Yeah."

"Fuckin' rights," goes Kenny. He's *hardening* the snowball now.

Harvey keeps smacking that fist into his palm. He horks up a big green one and lets it dangle from his lips before sucking it back up into his mouth again.

Wayne looks away.

"Could barely hit him, he's that skinny," goes Kenny.

Bobby says, "Built like a girl."

"Got a pussy, I bet," Kenny says.

Harvey snickers and Bobby goes, "Good one, Kenny," and The Meat brings his face even closer to Wayne's and says, "That true, Pumphrey? You really a chick?"

Wayne shakes his head, then tries lowering his arms, but again Pete tells him to keep them where they are.

"It's burning," Wayne says.

Pete looks back at the boys. "Listen to him: 'It's burning,' he says."

"That's the piss running down his leg," says Kenny.

"Yeah," Bobby says, "it's the piss."

Harvey's palm is red now from his own fist.

Pete focuses back on Wayne. Shakes his head. Clicks his tongue against his bottom teeth. "You go and piss yourself, Pumphrey?"

"No." Wayne's shoulders are about to catch fire. He's shaking from cold, or is it shame? Nose running. A dome of snot over the left nostril.

"Look at him, Pete," Kenny says. "Mommy didn't wipe his nose this morning."

Wayne goes to wipe but Pete digs a finger into Wayne's chest and tells him, for the last time, to keep *FUCKIN' STILL*. Then he says, "You're disgusting, Pumphrey. You're what's in the toilet bowl when I've eaten too many toutons."

Harvey and Bobby give each other high-fives.

Kenny tosses his snowball in the air and then catches it.

A school bus in the distance, the driver tiny behind the steering wheel. He slows as he approaches, veers right. Palms pressed against windows, squished noses and unhinged jaws, wide eyes. It rumbles by, a brief plume of exhaust left in its wake. Then silence. Four sets of eyes right on him. Wayne looks away, in the direction of the mine, then upwards where the mushroom cloud of iron ore dust hovers above it like a mistake. He imagines his father beneath that cloud somewhere, his hard hat tilted to the side and soot encrusted in his moustache, underneath his nails, between his teeth. What would his old man say about the raised arms and the snot and the school bus loaded with gawking children, he wonders.

Pete's voice brings him back. "What's his punishment gonna be?"

Bobby raises his hand.

"Yes, Bobby?" says The Meat.

"Kick him in the balls."

"Jesus Christ, Bobby, everything's balls with you." Pete looks over at the others. "Whaddya think, Kenny? What should Pumphrey's punishment be for walking ahead of us?"

Before Kenny can get his suggestion out, Wayne says, "I didn't know you were behind me."

Pete locks eyes with Wayne. "You arguing with me, Pumphrey?"

"Oh, you're dead, Pumphrey," goes Bobby. "Arguing with The Meat."

Tears in Wayne's eyes.

"Hey boys, get a load of this," goes Pete. "Little girl's crying."

"I'm not."

"No? What's that coming from your eyes then, Pumphrey? Cream of Wheat?"

Because wiping his cheeks would mean having to lower his arms, Wayne lets the tears roll down his face, onto his lips and tongue. He tastes salt and snot and remnants of the baloney and Honeycombs he had for breakfast.

"Tell you what," says Harvey.

"What?" goes Pete.

"I say me and Bobby hold 'em while Kenny throws that snowball he's making right at the little pussy's face, and if he so much as flinches we make him hump the snow like yesterday."

"Fuckin' rights," goes Kenny.

"Yeah!" Bobby shouts.

Pete shakes his head.

"Why not?" says Harvey.

"Because it's supposed to be *punishment*."

So much laughter now it almost seems to be shooting up from the ground, or falling from the sky. Bobby's clapping and Pete's holding his stomach and Kenny's just dropped his snowball and Harvey can barely breathe and Wayne starts running.

Now there's no sound other than his own heartbeat and a ringing in his ears and his boots thudding off the frozen street. The school's in the distance, shit-coloured against the grey morning, and he imagines sitting in a plastic chair and scribbling in a notebook and feeling safe for a moment, but then there's a load on him and he's falling and the wind's knocked out of him. And Bobby's bearing down all his weight and smirking and breathing, and Wayne wonders if the heavy boy has ever heard of Colgate.

"You're dead now, Pumphrey," says Bobby, "running from The Meat."

Wayne struggles to move. "I can't breathe."

Pete comes over and orders Bobby to get Pumphrey to his feet and hold him because Kenny's about ready to let his snowball rip.

Bobby stands him up, his fingers digging into Wayne's left arm. Harvey's got Wayne's right one.

Kenny's not six feet away, kicking at the ice to find some traction and chewing the inside of his cheek and furrowing his brow and squeezing the snowball in his hands, while Pete stands there like an umpire ready to either fly off the handle or pat a bottom. "Don't flinch, Pumphrey," he says, "this'll only take a second."

The school bell and then a skidoo's engine. Somewhere a barking dog.

Kenny lines up his shot. Gives Pete a look.

Pete nods.

Kenny draws in a big breath and lowers his chin into his chest.

Wayne imagines a broken nose or a black eye or, even worse, a concussion. He too draws in a breath and holds it, readying himself for impact. That's when he sees her walking towards them: jacket too small and wearing sneakers despite the icy street and no hat or mittens and her hair's messy and her cheeks are red.

Kenny draws back. Follows through—

She screams—

Kenny releases the snowball too soon, not enough torque, its trajectory slightly off course.

Wayne forces himself to stay still, to heed The Meat's warning, but then there's a cry beside him and Bobby drops and blood's staining the street.

# THREE

Bobby's on all fours searching for his tooth. "You don't suppose I swallowed it, do ya, Pete?" he says, his voice breaking.

Pete's too busy staring at Marjorie to answer. Marjorie with the dead father and who eats alone in the cafeteria and who, according to rumour, inserted a whole package of frozen Maple Leaf wieners up inside herself. A half-moon scar on her left cheek that they say she did *herself* to commemorate the cycle the moon was in when her father died.

Bobby's voice again. Steadier. "Found it!" He holds up the bloodied, rotted tooth. "Can they put her back in, Pete?"

Pete, his eyes still on Marjorie, says, "Once she's out she's out, dickwad."

Bobby stares at his tooth for ages, then puts

it in his pocket. Grabs a chunk of ice and presses it against his top lip. He glares at Kenny. "You're fuckin' cockeyed!"

"I got distracted." Kenny points at Marjorie and says, "Blame Maple Leaf."

Pete The Meat shoots Wayne a look. "Girlfriend showed up just in time, Pumphrey. Must be your lucky day, eh?" He tries in vain to stifle a laugh. "Not so lucky for Bobby though … he's just lost one of the *three* teeth he's got left."

Bobby takes the ice away from his mouth. His lip looks like a snake after it's swallowed a mouse. "It's not funny!"

"You're right, Bobby, it's not," Pete says.

Harvey can't stop smiling. "It *is* a little."

"Pete!"

"Easy, Bobby, Harvey's just foolin' with ya."

"Tell him to stop."

"Give it up, Harvey," Pete says. "How would you feel if you didn't have enough teeth to chew your food?"

Kenny says, "A custard diet soon enough."

Everyone laughs save for Bobby.

"Fuckers," Bobby says. He spits a glob of blood onto the street.

Another bus drives by.

Another school bell, too.

Everyone looks at Marjorie. She's long outgrown

her jacket, Wayne thinks. Why else would it cling to her like that? Doesn't even reach her waist.

Pete says, "How long you two been goin' out, Maple Leaf?"

Marjorie doesn't say anything.

The Meat steps closer. "Figured you'd try the real thing, eh?"

"Thank God," says Kenny. "My folks were getting sick and tired of going to Dominion and finding all the wieners gone."

Pete laughs. "Good one, Kenny."

She speaks then. "Leave Wayne Pumphrey alone."

Pete says, "Listen, boys, *IT* speaks."

Marjorie slips her hands into the back pockets of her jeans. "Can't find someone your own size to pick on?"

"How 'bout I pick on you?"

Wayne says, "Leave her alone," but when no one acknowledges he's said anything, it occurs to him he'd only mouthed the words.

"Big man, eh, Pete?" Marjorie says.

"That's right."

"You think you're something special, dontcha?"

"Mind your mouth, Maple Leaf."

"You're no different than the rest of us."

"No? I don't need the meat department at Dominion to get *laid,* do I? And I'm not a midget faggot like Pumphrey over there."

"*A midget faggot,*" Bobby repeats.

Marjorie pauses. "Is it true what I heard?"

The Meat smooths his almost-a-moustache again. "I don't know, Maple Leaf; what did you hear?"

Marjorie looks over at Wayne and then back at Pete. "That your real dad's not the one you live with."

Someone gasps: Harvey—no, Kenny, it's Kenny.

Bobby says, "You're in for it now, Maple Leaf."

The Meat stops blinking and his jaw goes slack and he licks his lips and swallows and looks right at Marjorie and says, "What did you say?"

Before Marjorie can repeat it, Kenny suggests that maybe it's best they go, but Pete tells everyone to stay put. "No, I want her to say it again. Come on, Maple Leaf, go ahead, or have you lost your nerve now?"

"Let's *go,* Pete—"

"*Shut up,* Kenny—"

"Your real dad's not the one you live with, I said."

So quiet.

"That, and you had a tough start."

Pete goes right up to Marjorie (close enough to kiss her if he puckered) and stares right into her eyes.

Wayne notices the thick fingers of Pete's right hand curling into a fist, so he moves towards him, then stops, and realizes he hasn't moved at all.

"You gonna strike a girl, Pete?" Kenny says.

"Don't know. Maybe."

Marjorie doesn't move.

Pete speaks again. "What about *your* real dad, eh Maple Leaf? Where's he? Oh right: rotting in some box."

It's like everything stops, or rather moves in quarter speed. The only way to process the words. *Rotting in some box,* that's exactly what The Meat said.

Marjorie stares at Pete with her sky-blue eyes that are the colour of Wayne's comforter. They're a commander's eyes after trudging through a field of slaughtered soldiers.

A gust of wind.

Snowflakes as big as peaches.

Kenny goes over and puts a hand on The Meat's shoulder. "Forget it, Pete. She's nothing."

No one says anything.

Pete slowly unfurls his fist and nods, and a sly grin lifts the corner of his mouth. "You're right, Kenny: she's nothing." Then to Marjorie, "How does it feel, Maple Leaf? To be no one? You're practically not even here." He laughs and the others laugh too, so he holds out his palm and Kenny slaps it and says, "Fuckin' rights."

"All right, boys, let's go," Pete says.

Bobby won't move.

"What's the matter?" Pete asks him.

"It's not fair: here I am with no tooth and what did Pumphrey lose?"

The Meat pauses, then says, "Oh, don't you worry about him, Bobby, he'll lose plenty. And more than a rotted tooth, too."

This seems to satisfy Bobby because he tries to smile, but it's too painful with his swollen lip, so he walks over and joins the others instead.

Pete looks at Wayne and says, "I'd watch my back if I were you," to which Bobby replies, "Thank God you're not, eh, Pete?"

"What?"

"Like Pumphrey."

Pete The Meat pauses for a moment. "Yeah, Bobby ... thank *God*."

# FOUR

Wayne's practically jogging to keep up with Marjorie. "Can't you slow down?" he says.

She doesn't answer, just keeps up her Olympic pace, chin tucked into her jacket collar, hands in her pockets, overly long strides as if there were endless potholes in her path she's trying to step over.

"I just wanted to thank you," says Wayne. "I appreciate what you did."

Suddenly she's down on her bum, legs splayed out like a fallen youngster on her first pair of skates. He rushes over and holds out his hand, but she won't take it.

"I'm not handicapped," she says, getting back to her feet and dusting away the snow on the back of her pants.

"Don't you have boots?" Wayne says.

"Does it look like it? You think I'd wear these if I didn't have to?"

Wayne doesn't say anything.

"Not all of us have rich dads working at the mine, Wayne Pumphrey."

Marjorie starts walking again and Wayne wonders how someone who always looks like he's just getting out of bed and who lives in a ratty coat with nicotine stains on the sleeves and who's forever in boots with untied laces could be rich. The rattling change in his father's pockets and his parents sometimes going into overdraft on their chequing account, so what's rich about that?

Wayne holds out his hands. "Would you like to borrow my mittens?"

She shakes her head.

"My toque? What's funny?"

"You want to be picked on less ... stop wearing that hat, Wayne Pumphrey."

"Really? What's wrong with it?"

"The ponies. The little piggies at the trough."

Wayne takes off the toque and looks at it. "Mom knit this."

"Exactly."

Marjorie turns to go.

"Wait."

"What now, Wayne Pumphrey?"

"Umm ..." He puts his toque back on. "Nothing."

"Just because I saved you doesn't mean we're going to be lifelong friends."

"Okay."

She starts to go again.

"Pete'll get you back for what you said. He hates anyone mentioning his real dad or his tough start and he struck a teacher once, I was told."

"Shouldn't believe everything you hear, Wayne Pumphrey." She stops and turns around. "Do you wear your sister's panties and listen to Rita MacNeil CDs?"

*"What?"*

"'Cause that's what *I've* been told."

"Well, it's a lie! I'd *never* wear my sister's panties!" Wayne pauses. "And they're my *mom's* CDs. I can't very well tell her to shut them off now, can I?"

Marjorie shrugs.

"What about what they say about *you?*" Wayne says.

"What about it?"

A rush of warmth in Wayne's face makes him turn away.

"My body, isn't it, Wayne Pumphrey? What's it to the crowd around here what I do with it."

Wayne doesn't speak.

"Let them talk. They're all so perfect, are they?"

A third school bell.

Then "Ode to Newfoundland."

Wayne sees late slips and wagging forefingers and lectures about responsibility and detention and staring out the window and wishing he were somewhere else.

"I hate Canning," Marjorie says. "At least if we lived on the island we could go to St. John's. Not everyone would know me. What? Why are you smiling?"

"'God's country,' Mom says."

"What, *Labrador?*"

"Yeah."

"Too cold for God in Canning."

"She says we have the best northern lights—"

"Pfft—"

"And that when the sky's blue and the sun's reflecting off the snow there's nowhere prettier."

"Really? Well you tell her that I can think of a hundred places better. A thousand."

"And the best of all, Mom says, is the quiet."

"That's because no one's stupid enough to live here. Except us."

Neither of them speaks for a long time. Then Wayne says, "Why does your mother always peek through the drapes?"

"I don't know, Wayne Pumphrey, why does your father always drive on the wrong side of the street?"

Because he knows there aren't always answers

for things, or at least ones that make sense, he stays quiet.

Then Marjorie says, "How long you gonna put up with it, Wayne Pumphrey?"

"Put up with what?"

"Whaddya think?"

He doesn't answer, listens instead to the faraway voices butchering the provincial anthem:

*When blinding storm gusts fret thy shore*
*And wild waves lash thy strand*
*Thro' spindrift swirl and tempest roar*
*We love thee, windswept land*
*We love thee, we love thee,*
*We love thee, windswept land*

Then he says, "Why'd you help?"

"Beats me."

"You've never before."

"Only so often you can walk past the same car wreck."

Wayne nods.

She brushes away the snow on her head.

"Pete shouldn't have said that," Wayne says. "About your dad."

She breathes and slides her hands into the back pockets of her jeans.

"Do you miss him?"

Marjorie doesn't say.

"Sorry. Perhaps I shouldn't have brought it up."

She turns around. Disappears into the sea of falling snow.

# FIVE

"You can take the paper bag off your head now, Mr. Pumphrey."

Wayne does, folding it neatly and laying it on his lap.

Mr. Rollie takes off his glasses and massages his eyes, then puts them back on. Runs a hand through his tangle of red hair. "Come closer, Mr. Pumphrey."

Wayne picks up his chair and goes over and positions it in front of the long table Mr. Rollie is sitting behind, then sits himself. He takes in the wall clock over the door with the stopped second hand and the whiteness of the room that's like a hospital or an insane asylum. The only colour is the orange of the plastic chairs and Mr. Rollie's hair and the brown food trays and the mural on the wall displaying the five basic food groups.

"You sure you wouldn't be happier in the band?" Mr. Rollie says.

"Tried, sir: the drums. Mrs. Cooper said I had no rhythm."

"She did, eh?"

"Mm-hm."

Mr. Rollie leans across the table. "It's just that I couldn't see your face."

"But that's the scene: Charlie Brown notices the cute girl staring and then puts a bag over his head."

"Yes, I'm well aware, Mr. Pumphrey, but it's important in auditions that the director sees what your mouth is doing. Your eyes."

"Should I try it again?"

"No, no."

Mr. Rollie twirls his pinky ring. His nails need trimming. "Didn't Mrs. Cooper let you try any of the other instruments?"

"Only interested in the drums."

Quiet for a moment.

"How old are you now, Mr. Pumphrey?"

"Fifteen."

"Right. You're small for your age, aren't you?"

"A little."

Mr. Rollie's pinky ring catches the cafeteria light and sparkles. "Perhaps it was your monologue choice. Most your age try stuff with a little more edge. Les Faulkner did a piece from *Glengarry Glen Ross*."

"What's Glengarry Glen Ross?"

"A David Mamet play."

"Who's he?"

"A famous American playwright."

"Oh."

"Yeah." Mr. Rollie crosses his legs and Wayne notices little William Shakespeares on his drama teacher's socks. "Lots of good drummers, were there? That why?"

"Jim Butt."

"Well, he's practically a prodigy. Other than Mr. Butt, I mean."

"A few."

"And they were all better than you?"

"Mm-hm." Wayne looks past Mr. Rollie's shoulder towards the main doors and sees Julie's face squished against the window. He looks away.

"I won't lie, Mr. Pumphrey, this year's production is going to require some really strong actors. Be nice to finally make the provincials. They're in St. John's this year."

"Really? Wow."

"You think you're ready for the drama club after what happened in the pageant last year, Mr. Pumphrey?"

"Yes, sir."

"You upset the manger."

"Costume was too big."

"And dropped the frankincense."

"Sweaty hands."

"You were pretty upset."

"I remember."

"You slipped out through the back." Mr. Rollie pauses. "There's more to acting than meets the eye, Mr. Pumphrey."

"I know."

"Do you?"

"Yes, sir: there're lines to memorize and pretty leading ladies to kiss or rescue or give mouth-to-mouth to—"

"Whoa, slow down, Mr. Pumphrey. Sounds like Hollywood's more your style."

"No sir, I don't care much for Hollywood. Who wants to be chased by paparazzi and photographed on the beach when you're not in the best of shape? No, a small school play suits me fine."

Mr. Rollie takes his glasses off again and puts one of the ears in his mouth. Chews. "You're a funny one, Mr. Pumphrey."

"Born too late, Mom says."

"Why does she say that?"

"On account I don't like the *Twilight* movies or Justin Bieber or iPhones or especially Facebook."

"Why especially Facebook?"

"Um ... no reason. Just some girl who pretended to like me and then posted how gross I was when I started to like her back."

Mr. Rollie lays his glasses down and slides back in his chair and folds his arms. After a long time he says, "What do you write in those notebooks of yours?"

"Hmm?"

"I've seen you ... in the cafeteria, the library, outside when the weather's nice, which isn't very often. Are they plays?"

"No."

"Short stories?"

"Letters."

"Letters?"

"Yeah, but they're mostly for me."

"For you?"

"That's right. I don't send them or anything."

"But aren't letters *meant* to be sent?"

"Not mine."

Mr. Rollie goes to say more but is interrupted by the opening door and Julie's poking-in head. "Sorry for barging in," she says.

"What is it, Miss Snow?"

"It's just that ... well, are you almost ready for me? Mom's waiting to take me to the shopping centre to get a skirt and we'd like to get there before it closes." Julie looks at Wayne and says, "There's others out here, you know."

"Miss Snow."

"Sorry, Mr. Rollie."

"If your skirt is more important than this term's production then maybe you should just go."

"No, sir, it isn't. I *really* want to be in the play (did I just hear you say the provincials were in St. John's this year?), it's just that I was planning on wearing the outfit to school tomorrow."

"I don't appreciate you listening by the door, Miss Snow, and I'm with someone right now, so wait your turn."

Julie shoots Wayne a glare. Squeezes her lips so tight they turn white. Slams the door.

"Sorry about that, Mr. Pumphrey."

"It's okay."

"Keeps the shopping centre in business, Miss Snow does."

"She *is* a snappy dresser."

Mr. Rollie glances up at the wall clock. "We should finish, Mr. Pumphrey. Anything else you'd like to add?"

"Not really, only that I'd like to be in the show because I think it might be nice to be a part of something."

Mr. Rollie sits there for a moment, then he puts his glasses back on and uncrosses his legs and gets to his feet. Holds out his hand.

Wayne shakes it.

"Thanks for coming in, Mr. Pumphrey."

"You're welcome."

Wayne makes his way to the door.

"Mr. Pumphrey?"

Wayne stops. "Yes, sir."

"You're far from gross."

"Thank you, sir, I appreciate it."

Wayne leaves.

# SIX

Supper's on the table when Wayne walks in: pea soup and dumplings, sliced homemade bread on a flower-patterned plate, cups of tea with swirling steam. A light above the stove illuminates the still-simmering pot, beside which rests the blackened wooden ladle that's always used for soups and sauces and macaroni and cheese and— for when his mother can't take much more of his father—throwing.

His mother is blowing on her loaded spoon, while his sister, Wanda, listens to her iPod. There's a place set for his father, but his father's not in it.

His mom slurps, then looks at Wayne and says, "Eat before it gets cold."

He goes over and sits down. His mother pours him a glass of milk. Lays a slice of bread beside his bowl.

Nickelback's wafting from his sister's side of the table, some song about a photograph and red eyes and a guy named Joey with something on his head.

His mother reaches over and yanks Wanda's earphones out.

"Hey!"

"Not at the table."

"Didn't have to tear my ears off—"

"How many times have I told you."

Wanda sits back and crosses her arms and stares into the living room as if the key to her escape might be there.

"Eat," his mother tells her, but Wanda won't, so his mother tells her again.

Wanda dips her spoon in, stirs, fills it, and then drops the contents back into the bowl. Repeats. Gives their mother a look as if to say, *I'm nearly eighteen and soon I'll be able to do whatever I fucking well want.*

Wayne blows on his own spoonful before putting it in his mouth. Hacks off a chunk of dumpling. Looks over at his dad's place, then at his mother. After a while he says, "Where is he?"

No one answers, so he says, "His soup'll get cold."

"Pfft," Wanda says.

Wayne looks across the table at her.

"Doubt he gives a shit about his soup right now."

"Wanda," his mother says.

"What?"

"You *know* what."

"Well how long does it take to pick up butter?"

No one says anything.

Wayne's mother drops another dumpling into his bowl even though he's not done with the first one.

"Where were you?" Wanda says.

He looks up. "School. You should try it."

"Funny. What were you doing at this thing called 'school'?"

"Auditioning."

"What?"

"For the play. Mr. Rollie says he needs really strong actors this year."

"Mr. Rollie? He's queerer than Sunday."

"Wanda," his mother says.

"Loves the young ones too, I'm told."

"Shut up," Wayne says.

"Don't drop your script."

"Mom!"

"Enough, Wanda!" his mother says.

Wanda laughs, bunched-together teeth in too small a mouth.

Then it goes quiet save for his mother's slurping. Afterwards she uses what's left of her doughboy to sop up the dregs in her bowl. Licks her fingers. Says to Wayne, "Your father's brother was an actor. Was on TV and everything."

"Uncle Philip?" Wayne says.

"Or he used to be anyway. Then he drove a truck, or was it a taxi? What odds, he's dead now."

"What shows?" Wayne says.

"Oh, goodness … I think he might have been in one about a wolf or a dog or something. *The Littlest Hobo,* I believe it was."

"Or, in Mr. Rollie's case, *The Littlest Homo,*" Wanda says.

Before Wayne can tell her to shut up, the sound of his father's car is in the driveway and everyone's suddenly adjusting themselves in their chairs: his mother pushing hers in, Wanda sitting a little more erect, and half of Wayne's bum off his own.

The engine dies and a car door opens, then closes.

"Don't say a word," his mother tells them.

Wanda goes to put her earphones back in, but his mother glares at her. Then she gets up and goes over to the stove and refills Wayne's bowl even though he didn't ask for more. She puts it down in front of him.

Boots on the porch. A hand on the door handle and a puff of air as it's pushed open. Footsteps. A cough. Something falls on the floor. Keys? Another cough. More footsteps. Closer. Past the foyer. Into the kitchen.

His father stands there: work shirt untucked beneath that nicotine-stained coat, woollen socks and strands of hair in his slits for eyes and soot in his moustache and a sway so slight it might not be happening at all.

He comes over and takes off his coat and drapes it across the back of his chair and sits down. Smoke and cold and iron ore dust coming off him.

Wayne's mother squeezes her tea bag. Adds milk. Stirs and stirs until there's a tornado inside her cup.

His father reaches for a slice of bread, dunking its corner into his soup. He takes a bite and scrunches up his face. "Freezing, this is."

Wayne's mother puts her cup down. "Been sitting there, hasn't it?"

"Could have left it in the pot."

"Supper's at five."

His father peers into his own teacup. "This isn't fit either, I suppose?"

Wayne's mother doesn't say anything.

Wayne's dad stands up and takes his soup over to the stove. Throws it in amongst the hot stuff, then refills his bowl. Comes back over. Nearly misses his chair upon sitting and sets everything shaking on the table. Wayne's milk spills over the sides of his tumbler and tea splashes onto the tablecloth. Wanda's able to cover her glass of Diet Coke just in time.

His father rights himself, then hovers over his
food and starts eating.

Wayne's mother rubs her forehead.

The grandfather clock chimes.

Finally, his mother says, "Where's the butter?"

Wayne slowly turns to look at his father. Wanda
does, too.

His father looks up from his bowl. Red eyes.
Brows slanted downward. Bits of soup entangled
in his moustache. On the verge of falling asleep it
looks like. He breathes in. Exhales. Glances around
the kitchen as if he's trying to remember where he
put something.

Wayne's mother goes, "'I'll pick some up,' that's
what you said, Calvin."

His father is still for a moment, then he drops his
spoon into his soup. Pushes the bowl aside and glares
across the table. "The minute I get in the door."

No one says anything.

"Just once I'd like to walk in and not have you
nag me."

Wayne's mother leans forward but doesn't
speak.

"You think Frank Hewitt up the street has to put
up with this every time he comes home ... What?"

"You're far from Frank Hewitt," Wayne's mother
says.

"Is that right?"

"I'm sure when Frank Hewitt tells his wife he's going to pick something up he bloody well comes back with it."

"I forgot."

"'I forgot,' he says. Don't forget the bar though."

Wanda pushes out her chair and leaves.

"Wouldn't forget the bar if you had Alzheimer's," his mother says.

Wayne clutches his glass just as his father swipes his own bowl onto the floor, flecks of pea soup striking Wayne's face.

Wayne's mother stands. "You've thrown your last bowl!"

"Have I now?"

She walks around the table—needing an extra-long stride to clear the broken bowl and spilled soup—into the hall. "That's the last bowl you'll ever throw!" A door slams. Then it goes quiet.

Wayne wipes his face and lets go of his glass and sees the imprint of his fingers.

His dad's staring in the direction of the hall. Then he turns and rests his face in his palms. After a while he lifts his head and looks at Wayne. "Do me a favour."

"Okay."

His father yawns and rubs his belly because his belly's always upset. Shifts closer. "Run to the store after you're finished and get some butter."

Wayne nods. His dad reaches over and messes his hair, then goes to pick up the broken bowl but Wayne does it for him, sweeping the shards into a dustpan and sopping up the pea soup with paper towels and then dropping it all into the garbage beneath the sink. He goes back over and sits down. Finishes his milk.

His father stares out the window.

"Mom says Uncle Philip used to be on TV," Wayne says finally.

His dad turns to him.

"Was in a dog show then drove a truck or was it a taxi?"

His father goes to pick up his mug but then remembers it's not fit for drinking. "It was a van. Showbiz people, mostly. Picked them up at the airport and drove them to their hotels or to movie sets."

A long silence.

Then Wayne says, "You've never mentioned it."

His father coughs and wipes his mouth and goes back to staring out the window.

"How about getting that butter now?"

Wayne nods. Walks to the foyer and gets into his jacket.

Dear Marjorie,

I just got in from picking up butter and was going to write my dad a letter because he threw the soup but I figured he's always throwing something so why not write to you instead since I hardly ever get saved and that's what you did today, you saved me, so thanks a lot.

You probably already know that Pete's been giving me a hard time ever since he moved here almost three years ago and everyone's afraid of him but you stood up to him and no one's <u>EVER</u> done that.

You're very brave and perhaps you could show ME how to be. I'm sorry that Pete said what he did. Are you okay? It must be hard to have a father that's dead. Who changes the light bulbs and takes out the garbage at your place?

I don't believe all that wiener stuff by the way. But even if it were true, what odds. Everyone does stuff, right? I do. Not all the time but mostly all the time. Do you ever worry about getting one lost up there? Is that even possible? Anyway, like you said, it's your body, right?

I don't suppose you'd want to be my friend? If not, I can just like you from a ~~distince~~ distance. You'll never have to know.

Thanks again, I really appreciate what you did.

Your friend from a distance,
Wayne Pumphrey

# SEVEN

It's been a week since the auditions and the cast list is posted just outside the cafeteria doors. Wayne's waiting for the lunchtime crowd to stampede in before taking a look. Mrs. Gambol, the home economics teacher—military stance and pulled-back hair and husky eyes—is there, and she's holding a boy by the back of the shirt and warning him about running and then making another student pull up his jeans, saying: "You think we all need to see your boxers, Martin?" Treena Cobb, who sits behind Wayne in math and constantly looks at his answers, is made to pull down her own T-shirt to cover the belly button ring and butterfly tattoo.

After everyone has gone in Wayne goes over and runs his finger down the list of names and stops at Marjorie's. He moves in and looks more closely.

It's her all right … playing Bonita Saunders, the
female lead. He continues down the list, then starts
over. Does it three more times, then pulls open the
cafeteria doors and goes inside.

At the counter he buys a hot dog, a carton of
milk (which he opens and takes a sip from right
away), and a bag of Crunchits, then makes his way
to an empty table near the window.

A foot belonging to Pete The Meat juts out
and trips him, but Wayne manages to stay upright,
spilling only a little milk onto his hot dog.

Pete's voice then. "Whoa there, Pumphrey.
Almost took a tumble, eh? Maybe keep your head
up instead of staring at your dicky bird."

Bobby laughs and says, "Surprised he can even
see it, eh, Pete?"

"Good one, Bobby," says The Meat.

"Hey, Pumphrey?" shouts Harvey.

Wayne turns.

Harvey holds up a French fry and says, "See this
here fry? That's you." Harvey tears the fry in two and
then squishes each piece and Kenny—now getting
the idea—grabs the ketchup bottle and squeezes
and it shoots out and he says, "That's *your* blood,
Pumphrey."

Wayne keeps on walking.

Up ahead, Julie gives him a dirty look and points
a macaroni-filled fork at him and says, "All that time

you spent in the audition and you *still* didn't get a part in the play."

He continues on, letting her laughter fade behind him, towards the table where the volley-ball players sit. No high-fives, or glances even. Past the rebellious table with the berets and dreadlocks, painted nails and combat boots. Lips and noses and corners of eyelids pierced. Past the overachievers' table with their erect backs and nice sweaters, open textbooks and laptops, too-neat haircuts and expensive glasses.

Finally Wayne arrives at the empty table. What to call it? he wonders. He sits and takes a napkin and soaks up the milk on his hot dog. Rips open his Crunchits and puts a few in his mouth. *The Going-It-Alone Table,* he thinks. He swallows and takes a sip of what milk there is left. *The Nobody Table.* He reaches inside his knapsack and takes out his notebook and a Razor Point extra-fine pen.

Dear Nobody Table,

Thanks for being free 'cause I don't know where else I would have sat. Nearly got tripped by Pete on the way over and now my hot dog is soaked but I don't mind 'cause I often dunk my toast in my milk anyway so what's the difference?

Julie's looking at me right now and she's sticking her index finger into her mouth and pretending to throw up and everyone's laughing and I guess it is kinda funny because she's so committed to it.

Bobby's smirking at me and miming that he's masturbating and Kenny's pretending he's throwing a snowball and Pete's nodding and smoothing his almost-a-moustache and Harvey keeps tearing his French fries and I feel like standing up and throwing my tray and saying, All right, I get it, you can STOP NOW! I just won't look up at anyone from now on, although it's hard not to when you know you're being stared at. Oops, just looked up again. I'll start over. Okay, that's better.

So I didn't get a part in the play and I don't think I overlooked my name because I stared at the cast list for ages and how long does it take to find your name if it's written down somewhere? Les's is there of course 'cause how can it not be seeing as he did a monologue from that American play and he's been in drama forever and has already started looking into acting schools in Toronto and Montreal when he graduates next year. Paul Stool's on the list, which is surprising because he's always got an erection that he hides behind books and lockers and desks and sometimes he just lies there on his stomach and he says it's so he can rest his back but everyone knows that lying on your stomach does just the opposite. Sharon's on the list too and I don't know how she'll do it without a Snickers. If she's not eating one she's dreaming about one or asking for change so she can buy one from the machine or here in the cafeteria. And she won't share either, just crams the whole thing in her mouth like it's ~~oxegen~~ oxygen. Julie's on the list but she's not playing the female lead which is another reason she looks so mad, I bet, and you'll never guess who is. You'll never be able to, not in a million years. Give up? All right, I'll tell you. MARJORIE POPE, that's who. Can you believe it? I didn't even know she liked drama and I'm pretty sure she's never been in anything before and it's not like she says a whole lot so how's she gonna stand up in front of everyone and say all those lines? Oops, I just looked up again and her ears must be burning because it's her—

"Since when do you sit here?" Marjorie says. She's holding a half-eaten apple.

"There was nowhere else."

"This is my spot."

"It is?"

"Yeah. *Today*."

Wayne closes his notebook and thinks he's finally come up with a name: *The Nobody-Is-Allowed-To-Sit-Here-But-Marjorie Table.*

"Tomorrow it might be over there," Marjorie adds, "the next day ... somewhere else. Slip in, slip out. That's how I prefer it." She glares at him for a long time.

He starts gathering his things.

"Well … seeing as you're already here," she says.

Wayne lays his tray back down. "Thanks. Appreciate it."

She sits opposite him and takes a bite of her apple.

"That all you're eating?" Wayne says.

She doesn't answer. Just chews.

"It's not very much. Want a Crunchit?"

"What, that processed shit?"

"They're only Crunchits."

"Won't be 'only Crunchits' when you've got colon cancer."

Wayne pushes the bag aside. Grabs his hot dog. "Guess you don't want a bite of this then."

"Rather eat rat shit."

He lays the hot dog down. "Sometimes I'll sit with my sister, Wanda, but she skips most days lately. Hey, congratulations by the way."

"For what?"

"The play; whaddya think?"

"What are you talking about, Wayne Pumphrey?"

"Didn't you see the cast list?"

Marjorie bites her apple. Shrugs.

"You're playing Bonita Saunders. Les is playing your husband."

Marjorie can't seem to swallow what's in her mouth. She sucks in a breath and says, "Did it on a whim. Wasn't expecting to get anything."

"More than 'anything'—the *lead*."

Marjorie looks at the ceiling.

Wayne says, "Didn't see you at the auditions."

She stays quiet.

"I said I didn't see you at the auditions—"

"I heard you."

Wayne waits.

Finally Marjorie says, "Waited till everyone was gone now, didn't I. Mr. Rollie was locking up."

"How come?"

"I don't know. Wasn't sure I wanted to go through with it."

"Why did you?"

"You ask a lot of questions, Wayne Pumphrey."

"Sorry."

They say nothing for a long time, the floor vibrating from the hum of hundreds of voices all trying to talk over one another and laughing and scheming about ways to acquire their weekend liquor.

Pete's looking over, Wayne notices, and he's grinning and pushing his index finger in and out of a hole he's made with the opposite hand.

Wayne turns away.

It's not until Marjorie's apple is a core that she speaks again, and what she says is: "It'll get me out of the house."

Wayne stares at her. "Hmm?"

"You asked me why and I'm telling you it'll get me out of the house."

"Oh." Then, after a while, "You don't like your place?"

Marjorie doesn't say whether she does or doesn't.

He puts some Crunchits in his mouth and tries chewing while blocking out visions of colon tumours and chemotherapy and falling-out hair. Manages to swallow.

"Are *you* on the list?" she says.

Wayne shakes his head.

She puts her core on his tray. "Better off. Why walk through a hail of bullets if you don't have to, right?"

"Huh?"

"Pete. He'd never give you any peace then."

Wayne stares in the direction of The Meat and his posse, then looks back at Marjorie and says, "Doesn't give me any *now*."

"Yeah well, it'd be worse if you were in the play."

"What, so I'm supposed to do nothing for the rest of high school because of Pete?"

Marjorie doesn't answer right away, then she says, "It'd be easier."

"But *you're* doing the play."

"Big difference between you and me."

"And what's that?"

Marjorie straightens up in her chair and says, "I couldn't give a shit, that's what, but you … you take things to heart."

"How would you know? You haven't so much as grunted at me in all the years you've lived up the street."

"And you've gone out of your way to talk to *me*? Don't think I never noticed how you'd always speed up whenever I was walking behind you, or slow down whenever I was ahead."

"And don't think *I* never noticed all those times you passed by while I was being put into a headlock or given a wedgie or whatever."

Marjorie stares at her fingers.

Wayne fiddles with his Crunchit bag.

Then Mrs. Gambol reappears from across the room and goes over to Pete's table and points her finger at Bobby, and whatever she says makes the colour drain from Bobby's face. Harvey and Kenny try not to laugh.

Students begin leaving.

"I kept my distance because I was embarrassed," Wayne says at last. "Why would you want to talk to the guy that eats yellow snow?"

Quiet for a moment, then Marjorie says, "I keep the meat department at Dominion in business, remember, so I could ask you the same question."

Wayne looks towards a gang of girls in short skirts and long boots, one of whom is Julie, as they exit the cafeteria in a clump of twisting heads and whispers and finger pointing. Wayne also notices Pete The Meat and his posse getting to their feet. Pete punches Bobby in the shoulder, and when Bobby shrugs and gives The Meat a look as if to say *What was that for?* Pete punches him again.

The volleyball team's suddenly on their feet, patting each other's bottoms and pumping their fists into the air in anticipation of this evening's game, while the crowd at the alternative table compare tattoos and body piercings. The overachievers are cramming the last bit of work into what time there is left, glued to their computer screens like porn addicts.

Marjorie says, "You ever get tired?"

"Of what?"

"Of being Wayne Pumphrey?"

"I don't know. You ever get tired of being Marjorie Pope?"

Marjorie looks away, then at her fingers again. "Sometimes."

"Me too," says Wayne. He breathes in and lets it out and says, "But I can't not be me, right? And you can't not be you."

She shrugs.

A bell rings.

"I'm sorry about last week," Wayne says. "I shouldn't have brought up your dad."

For a second Marjorie looks about ready to pull another disappearing act, but instead she stays put and says, "The answer is yes, I do. Wouldn't you miss yours?"

Wayne imagines life without his father: no smell of tobacco and aftershave and no empty lunch box on the counter and no coughing or used tea bags in the sink and no hands messing his hair and no knocked-over garbage cans when his father goes to park the car. He looks up at Marjorie and nods.

Thighs as sturdy as light poles beside him now and the smell of skin cream strong enough to disintegrate nose hairs. Mrs. Gambol, hands on her hips and a slight bend in one knee, says, "You two planning on staying all afternoon?"

Wayne looks around the room and wonders when it was that the place had cleared out. He stares back at Mrs. Gambol. "We're just leaving, Miss."

Mrs. Gambol scrutinizes Wayne's still-full tray. "Perhaps if you ate more you wouldn't be so small."

Wayne gets to his feet and notices that Marjorie is already near the double doors. He goes to catch up, but the teacher's voice stops him.

"Your tray."

Wayne grabs it and throws out the food and

stacks the tray with the others. Makes his way across the floor.

"Pick up the pace," Mrs. Gambol says. "The world's not going to wait, you know."

# EIGHT

Here's the rest of Wayne's day: en route to geography from biology, an unknown assailant knocks his books from his hand. Then, while sitting in chemistry, Jeff Hibbs lets one go and blames him. Everyone, including Julie, covers their noses while Mr. Bolan asks if anyone can name the primary gas released in Wayne's fart and Jeff says: gay gas and Mr. Bolan says: no, nitrogen. In English, a drawing is passed to Wayne depicting a dwarfish stick man being decapitated by a muscular man (Pete). The caption, grammatically incorrect and in bold letters, reads: **YOUR DEAD PUMPHREY!!!** And finally, standing in front of his locker at the end of the day, Bobby comes and pins him up against it and warns him to watch out for Pete The Meat and then threatens to yank out one of Wayne's teeth to make up for the one Bobby

lost. Then Bobby walks down the corridor towards
the double doors and, before pushing them open,
gives Wayne the finger.

For the longest time Wayne just stands there
while the rest of the students turn combination locks and put on coats and throw books into
knapsacks and tear off into what's left of the day
like finally freed prisoners. That's when he notices
Corey Parrot, six lockers down, fiddling with his
lock that never wants to open.

Wayne watches for a while, then says, "Want me
to try?"

Without so much as a glance, Corey shakes his
head. Tries the combination again. Nothing.

"It's twice around clockwise then—"

"Buzz off," Corey says. He tries again. Still won't
open.

The hall's deserted now, so Wayne walks down
to where Corey is, but Corey sticks out his palm as
if to say, *Stay where you are,* so Wayne does.

"Suppose I know how to open my own lock."
Corey turns the dial slowly, pauses, then yanks.
Nothing. He curses.

"Let me," Wayne says.

"*No!*" Corey looks up and down the corridor,
then back at Wayne. "Didn't I tell you to buzz off?"

Wayne doesn't say anything.

Again Corey scans the hallway, then takes a step

in Wayne's direction. "And stop calling my house."
He's whispering now. "Can't you take a hint?"

Wayne stays quiet.

"I don't want to be a jerk, but you leave me no
choice— What? Stop staring at me like that—like
you don't know what's what. Pete said if I hung
out with you he'd rip out my braces, *okay*? Make *me*
hump the snow too, and my dad's foreman so what
do you think he'd say?"

Silence.

"You'd do the same thing, Wayne ... if you were
me." Corey pauses, then points at his own mouth.
"Plus I'm getting these off soon and Monica said I
might not be too bad looking and she'd consider
being my girlfriend, so you see the position I'm in.
Why should we *both* suffer?"

Somewhere a phone rings.

Corey's finally able to open his lock. "See, told
you I knew how."

Wayne walks back to his own locker and gathers
his things and Corey says,

"I'm sorry but I can't change it, can I?"

Wayne gets into his jacket. Grabs his toque and
is about to put it on but remembers what Marjorie
said, so he stuffs it in his pocket instead.

"If he ever lets up on you," Corey says, "we can
be friends again. Okay?"

"Okay."

Corey's receding footsteps and the doors being pushed open and then slamming shut and the silence afterwards like spreading pain.

Wayne closes his locker and walks down the hall and is just about to leave when suddenly he hears clicking shoes and a voice that's Mr. Rollie's saying, "One moment, Mr. Pumphrey! One moment!"

Wayne turns around and waits for his drama teacher to catch up.

"So glad I caught you," Mr. Rollie says, putting his hands on his hips like he's out of breath. He takes a moment and then says, "Guess you saw the cast list, huh?"

Wayne nods.

"I'm sorry."

"It's all right. *You're a Good Man, Charlie Brown* was a bad choice."

"No, it wasn't. It's more that you look so young. And you're quite a bit smaller than everyone else. I needed blocky actors who could look like miners."

"Like Paul Stool?"

"Mm-hm. And Shane Brody and Jason Buckle."

"What about Les? He's not blocky."

"No, but he *is* the best actor in the school. Although Miss Pope might give him a run for it. I don't think I've ever seen an audition so authentic." Then, "Do you know her?"

"She lives up the street from me, but not really."

"Well, with her and Les I think we have a real shot at making the provincials in St. John's."

"That's great."

Quiet for a moment.

Wayne zips up his jacket. "Well, I better get home."

"Hang on, Mr. Pumphrey."

Wayne stays where he is.

Mr. Rollie lays a hand on Wayne's shoulder. "I was thinking maybe you could help me direct."

Wayne doesn't say anything.

"That means you and I will discuss the scenes and then tell the cast how to go about making them work. It'll be up to us where they stand and where they walk and what lighting will work best. We'll have a say about the set, too, and the music. Will we have the school band play live or have everything pre-recorded, for instance? The whole production will be you and me, Mr. Pumphrey." He pauses. "How does that sound?"

Wayne looks down at Mr. Rollie's pointy shoes, then back up. "Does anyone see the director?"

Mr. Rollie uses his pinky to push up his glasses. "Well, no, but the whole thing is the product of the director's imagination. Name your favourite movie."

Wayne thinks for a moment. "I don't know, *Avatar*—no, *The Lord of the Rings*. No, wait, *The Hangover*."

"Really?"

"Mm-hm."

"Okay. Well Wayne, behind that film was a director who made it all happen. They're the leaders, the train conductors, pilots of the 747s, sergeants of the battalions, Bill and Melinda Gates, Steve Jobs, Sidney Crosby. That's why I chose you: because you're a leader. You have that creative mind, Mr. Pumphrey. That imagination. If you're brave, one day you'll discover it's your greatest gift."

Wayne breathes in. Sees himself sitting behind that long table with Mr. Rollie telling Julie where best to stand; Marjorie how best to deliver that line; the drummer, Jim Butt, the best time at which to strike the cymbal.

"Well, Mr. Pumphrey?"

Wayne looks up and nods. "All right."

Mr. Rollie claps his hands. "Wonderful. We'll make a fine team, you and I." He holds out his hand.

Wayne shakes it.

"Tomorrow we'll begin."

"Okay."

"We'll have twelve weeks of rehearsal, so there'll be no time to waste if we want to make the provincials."

"Okay."

They let go hands.

Wayne turns to leave.

"Mr. Pumphrey?"

Wayne stops. "Yes, sir?"

The drama teacher reaches into his pocket and takes out a piece of paper and unfolds it and hands it to Wayne and Wayne looks at it for ages.

"Well?" Mr. Rollie says at last.

"Well what?"

"Does it look like me?"

Wayne shrugs. "A little. Around the eyes."

"You think so? Hmm. I'd never wear a sequined dress, though, or get my nose pierced. And I certainly wouldn't say that awful thing they have me saying."

Wayne pauses. "Who did it?"

"I was hoping *you* could tell me."

Silence.

"I don't know."

Mr. Rollie takes the drawing back. "Flattering though, isn't it? Someone going to all that trouble to draw a likeness of me." He puts the picture back in his pocket. "High school won't last forever, Mr. Pumphrey."

Wayne nods. Walks out into the cold dark.

———

Dear Mr. Rollie,

Are you sure you meant to call ME a leader?

Only 'cause I don't much feel like one. I mean, Barack Obama is a leader and Bill and Hillary Clinton and Jean Chrétien and Stephen Harper and Nelson Mandela and Oprah Winfrey and Sidney Crosby and Georges St-Pierre, but ME? How can someone who eats alone and walks alone and writes these letters alone be a leader? Leaders ought to be fearless and charming and good-looking (Okay, scratch Stephen Harper) and snappy dressers, but me … I'm fearful and awkward and far from a catch and my style won't be in any magazine.

Shouldn't leaders have a look in their eye and be able to sway a crowd and get people talking and erase the ~~deficeit deficient deficiet~~ deficit and pin their opponents and score the winning goals and take good pictures? Have you ever seen my grade nine photo? Not pretty.

Leaders can talk to anyone and they shake thousands of hands (I've hardly shaken any) and they have their own production companies and magazines and they run the White House and Parliament and what have I run other than away?

I'm sorry, Mr. Rollie, but I think you made a mistake. I'm no leader. And I think the only reason you made me co-director was because you felt bad, but I'll take the job anyway because it's good to have somewhere to go and something to do and someone other than the wall to look at and say stuff to.

Thanks for showing me the drawing someone did of you. It never occurred to me to look at it as flattering, so thanks for helping me see things in a different light.

You're gay, aren't you? My sister says you are because you wear pointy shoes and have a pinky ring, but what odds if you are? Sure there's this big lesbo chick in Wanda's grade twelve class who has a girlfriend and they hold hands and kiss in public and everything.

Is that man who sometimes waits for you in the parking lot after school your boyfriend? Will you get married? Are you considering adopting? If there were a parade in Canning would you guys march in it?

Your co-director who's far from a leader,
Wayne Pumphrey

# NINE

It's almost suppertime. Wayne's supposed to be
shovelling the driveway like his father asked, but
instead he's leaning on the shovel, staring up the
road at the police car and the ambulance parked
in Marjorie's driveway. Swirling lights, running
engines, clouds of exhaust like doughboys. Across
the street, he notices the Galbraiths gawking
through their living room window. Mr. Galbraith
is shirtless, his gut hanging over the waist of his
track pants as he holds a tub of what looks to be ice
cream, which his wife and youngest daughter are
digging into with long spoons. Their oldest, Natalie,
is talking into a cell phone, giving the play-by-play
to some girlfriend she'll probably meet tomorrow
by the water fountain, Wayne thinks, just before
spreading the news to the whole school. Two
houses down on Wayne's side of the street stands

Miss Flynn, twice divorced, and not long back from
St. John's with her new teeth and flatter tummy and
less pointy chin. A parka over her flannel pyjamas
and a cigarette jammed between Botoxed lips. She
shakes her head at Wayne and, without taking out
her smoke, says, "What in God's name is goin' on
up there?"

Wayne doesn't know, so he stays quiet and turns
back to Marjorie's. Miss Flynn's voice behind him
then, saying, "There's an ambulance, so it's probably
not good. Hope it's not the young one."

Marjorie's front door swings open revealing
two paramedics and they're pushing a gurney and
someone's on it. Marjorie? He moves closer. Stops.
No, her mother. Strapped down. Why?

"Who is it?" Miss Flynn wants to know. "The
girl?"

Marjorie's mother starts shouting and cursing
and trying to break free from her restraints.

"Thank God," Miss Flynn says, "I thought it was
the young one."

The paramedics wheel Marjorie's mom to the
rear of the ambulance. The shorter and balder
one shouts, "On the count of three," so they count
and lift and then hoist Marjorie's mother into the
back like an old refrigerator. Then the one who'd
suggested counting hops in the back with her, while
his partner goes and gets in the driver's side.

"What's wrong with her, do you think?" Miss Flynn says.

Commotion from the Galbraiths' place, Wayne notices. Mr. Galbraith has dropped the ice cream and is getting an earful from his wife. Their youngest is crying and their oldest is shouting something while pointing to her phone.

Then Marjorie's in the doorway and she steps out onto the porch and she's got her hand over her mouth. A woman cop's beside her, hat in one hand and a little notebook in the other, k.d. lang haircut and fit looking. The officer puts her hat back on and closes her notebook and says something, which makes Marjorie run back inside.

"First her father, now this," Miss Flynn says.

The cop waits on the porch and stares at the sky and her breath is like steam from a kettle.

Everyone's pressed against the window at the Galbraiths' now and it's a wonder they haven't burst through the glass. Flattened faces and palms and Mr. Galbraith's belly button and stomach and nipples and someone should really tell him to put on a shirt.

Marjorie comes back out and she's got her jacket and she zips it up and closes the door and follows the cop to the back of the ambulance and the shorter and balder paramedic offers his hand and helps her inside. The cop closes the door and walks back to her cruiser and gets in and Wayne notices her talking into a handheld radio.

The ambulance backs out of the driveway and takes off up the street, its lights going but no sound, and then the police car is pulling out and following it and soon they've rounded the corner and are gone and it's suddenly so quiet that Wayne thinks he might be all alone in the world, but then Miss Flynn reminds him he isn't by saying, "Not all there, that woman."

Wayne turns around.

"Ever since her husband died." Miss Flynn's cigarette is nearly burned down to the butt, so she flicks it into the snow and says, "Some people never get over things."

No one in the window of the Galbraiths' now, save for handprints and the outline of Mr. Galbraith's gut.

"Divorce is like death, they say," goes Miss Flynn. Then, "Not for me. I was relieved."

Now he's shovelling without any memory of having started and he's thinking about what Miss Flynn said about some people never getting over things. After some time he hears her say,

"Got a bone to pick with you."

He stops and looks at her.

"Do you know what this cost?"

"Oh, sorry. You look good, Miss Flynn."

"Well, the swelling hasn't completely gone down yet, but it's nice of you to say all the same. Foolishness I'm sure, at my age, but what odds. It makes me feel better, doesn't it?"

Wayne looks back up the street towards Marjorie's place, at the drawn curtains and all the lights out, and wonders if anyone ever lived there at all. When he turns back around, Miss Flynn is gone, as is the light on her porch. Then there's a voice and it's his father's saying, "That's all you've done?" And, "Should have done it myself." The door slamming and that silence again and this time Wayne's *sure* of it: he *is* alone in the world.

—

Dear Marjorie,

Is your mom going to live? I hope so or you'll be an orphan. Do you have relatives you can stay with till you're eighteen?

Did you see me gawking? Dad said it's nobody's business but Mom said, What, we're supposed to pretend the woman wasn't taken away in front of the whole street?

Here's me wanting to be taller and braver and more popular and I bet all you want is for your mom to be okay— Oh, hold on a sec someone's knocking on my door—

"Still awake?" his mother says.

"Yeah."

The door opens and his mother pokes her head in. "You asked me to let you know if they came back and they have."

"You sure?"

"Arm in arm up the porch steps, although I think it was more the young one making sure her mother didn't fall." His mom pauses. "Since when did you care about them up the road?"

Wayne looks away. "I'm helping Mr. Rollie direct and Marjorie's one of our lead actors, so what would we do without her?"

"I see. Well, they're back, so no need to worry."

"Okay."

Quiet.

"What were you writing?"

Wayne lays his palm over the page. "Nothing."

"Okay. Goodnight."

"Goodnight."

His mother leaves and Wayne listens to her fading-away footsteps and her opening another door and then the silence. He takes his hand away from the page and writes:

Mom just told me that your mom's all right and I can't tell you how relieved I am! Probably not as relieved as you though, eh? What happened anyway?

She's not sick, is she? Hope it's not cancer or anything because Mom says that cancer is everywhere and even the young ones are dropping like flies. Anyway I'm glad she's back and that you can go on living up the street.

Oh, by the way, I was meaning to say that Mr. Rollie asked me to be assistant director. He says I can tell people how to say their lines if they're not saying them right and I can help him with the script and things. Not too sure what I think about it 'cause I only wanted a part and what do I know about directing? But Mr. Rollie seems to think I can do it. He says I'm a leader only I don't know it yet (ha ha ha)!!! Don't know about that! I said I'd do it because it might be nice to be a part of something. Is that why you're doing it?

You might find this weird but I write these letters to say to people what I don't have the courage to say in real life. I've been doing it for a long while now and I've filled tons of notebooks. I suppose if anyone ever read what I've written I'd have to leave town.

I should go to bed now but I'll just say that sometimes I feel like there's no sense in anything. Do you?

Your friend who feels like there's no sense in anything,
Wayne Pumphrey

# TEN

Marjorie finishes her monologue and turns to Les Faulkner, but Les can't seem to remember what comes next. In the script he's supposed to go to Marjorie's character, Bonita, and kiss her cheek and wrap his arms around her, but it's like he's lost the capacity to move. Those sitting on the other side of the room look frozen, too. Wax figurines. Sharon's got a Snickers in her mouth, but she's not chewing; Paul Stool is actually sitting up with nothing over his crotch (cured at last); Julie Snow is on her knees about to apply a fresh coat of watermelon lipstick; and Shane and Jason have stopped drawing tits and vaginas and dicks on their scripts.

Mr. Rollie slides forward in his chair and wipes his eyes beneath his glasses and swallows and looks at the wall clock and tells everyone that that's enough for today and we can go home.

The cast needs a moment more to remember how to blink, breathe, stand up and put one foot in front of the other, swing their arms, and finally exit through the double doors.

Mr. Rollie calls Marjorie back.

She comes over and takes her place in front of the long table. Odd socks and too-short jeans and electrical tape over the toe of one sneaker. Bangs in her eyes and she's chewing on her cheek and her legs are crossed at the ankles like she needs to pee.

Mr. Rollie takes off his glasses and sets them on the table and looks at Marjorie. "Just wanted to say you were exceptional just now, Miss Pope."

Marjorie doesn't say anything.

"Mr. Faulkner was a little thrown, but at least now he'll know he can't coast along as usual." Mr. Rollie pokes Wayne in the shoulder. "What did you think, Mr. Pumphrey?"

Wayne lays down his Razor Point extra-fine pen. "Awfully good."

Mr. Rollie nods. "Wasn't it?"

Wayne turns to Marjorie. "Better than the Hollywood crowd even."

Mr. Rollie offers Marjorie a chair but Marjorie won't sit. He twirls his pinky ring for ages and then says, "I don't see how we *couldn't* make the provincials now. They won't know what to make of you in St. John's."

Marjorie slips her hands into her back pockets. Stares at something on the floor.

"All this time," Mr. Rollie says, "passing you in the corridors, having you in my English classes. Last year you were so quiet I forgot you were even there. And now *this*."

"Awfully good," Wayne says again.

"Where does it come from, Miss Pope, your mother's or your father's side?"

Marjorie looks up and then down at the floor again and Wayne feels something seep from the room.

Mr. Rollie shifts in his chair and says, "I'm sorry, Miss Pope, I shouldn't have asked—"

"Certainly not my mother's," Marjorie says. "She freezes up talking to the bank teller. So I guess my dad's side. He was real into music, especially Radiohead, and he loved movies and even tried to write a screenplay."

A long silence.

"Your guidance counsellor will hate me," Mr. Rollie says at last, resting his chin on cupped hands, "but I think it's your calling."

Wayne writes "calling" down in his notebook.

"For me it's to teach English and drama and direct school plays. Mr. Inkwell's destiny is to be principal, and old Mr. Ricketts is there to make sure the heat works in winter and that we have lights to do our work without straining our eyes." Mr. Rollie picks his glasses up and chews on one of the ears. "Some people have trouble finding their calling. Others not so much. What's important is to never stop searching." He sits back and stares at the ceiling and for a moment seems lost, but then he sits forward again and puts his glasses on and smiles with his teeth that are almost like baby ones and says, "You both ought to be going now, it's nearly suppertime."

Marjorie says goodbye and leaves while Wayne collects his things.

"The chivalrous thing would be to walk with her," says Mr. Rollie, "it being dark and everything."

"I would, except she walks so fast. Always a step ahead."

Mr. Rollie rests a hand on Wayne's shoulder and says, "Then you'd better catch up, hadn't you?"

# ELEVEN

Wayne bends over and offers his outstretched hand to Marjorie, but she doesn't take it.

"I'm not an invalid, Wayne Pumphrey," she says, getting back to her feet.

"It's those sneakers," Wayne says.

Marjorie brushes the snow off her backside.

"You need boots."

"Gonna buy them for me, Wayne Pumphrey?"

He doesn't say anything.

Marjorie starts walking again.

He tries to keep up. After a while he goes, "How can you walk so fast?"

Nothing for a moment, then her saying, "I pretend Mom's behind me."

"What?"

"Never mind."

For a long time they walk and say nothing, their footsteps crunching beneath them. Clouds for breath.

Then Wayne says, "Five o'clock and it's already dark."

Marjorie mumbles something and Wayne doesn't catch it so he asks her to say it again and she goes, "I said, it never gets warm here."

"What do you expect for January."

"January ... April ... *every* month. It snowed in July last year."

"Did it?"

"It's like living in the North Pole."

They continue on, Wayne stealing glances at the northern lights and the millions of stars and the quarter moon.

The sound of a skidoo in the distance.

A dog barks.

"Mr. Rollie cried," Wayne says finally. "During your monologue."

Marjorie just keeps going.

"Sharon, too, I think. Or else she was choking on her Snickers."

Marjorie puts her hands in her pockets and tucks her chin downwards and walks even faster.

"Paul Stool lost his hard-on—not that I was looking or anything, but sometimes it's impossible not to."

"No girl wants to hear that, Wayne Pumphrey …
even if it *is* Paul Stool."

"No, it was a compliment, you were so good you
took his mind off it."

She nearly slips again, but manages to stay
upright.

"And I meant what I said too about you being
better than the Hollywood crowd."

She says nothing. Turns left onto Lakeside Drive.

He follows and, after a while, says, "You're
better than Angelina Jolie."

She stops and turns around.

He stops too.

"I know my own way home," she says.

"The chivalrous thing would be to walk you."

For a moment they stand staring at each other,
then Marjorie says, "Saw you gawking the other
night, by the way. Gawk, gawk, gawk, that's all
anyone around here is good for."

"I didn't mean to." Wayne pauses. "She okay?"

Marjorie looks away. "She'll know to cut the
beef in smaller chunks from now on."

"What?"

She stares back at him. Slips her hands into her
back pockets again. "For the stew, I mean. Piece
lodged in her throat. Did the Heimlich thingy, but it
didn't work. The hospital's only five minutes away,
but it still took the ambulance forever."

"Oh."

She heads off again and he follows again.

A man passes pulling a child on a toboggan.

Sometime later Wayne hears faraway laughter, so he turns and, through a front window, sees people gathered around a kitchen table playing cards and drinking from tumblers and pointing and holding their stomachs. Through another window in another house Wayne notices a woman sitting alone by firelight: long hair and her feet on an ottoman, her toes extended—like a ballerina—towards the flame. Up ahead, a cat scoots across the road, finding refuge beneath a parked SUV. Music somewhere: guitars and mandolins. A harmonica? A cloud, or is it iron ore dust drifting in front of the moon?

At the intersection of Balsam and Oak, Marjorie stops.

Wayne comes up beside her.

No one talks for ages.

Marjorie fixes her gaze on the tiny bungalow with the closed drapes on the corner. At last she says, "Sometimes I hate going in."

"Why?"

"None of your business *why* ... I just *do*."

He pauses. "I hate going home sometimes, too."

"Pfft."

"What?"

"Nothing."

Silence.

Wayne says, "Mom threatens to leave all the time."

"Oh yeah? Does she sit in front of the curtains all day and night in her bathrobe and not eat and not brush her teeth?"

"No. But she does pack her suitcase a lot. Even *goes* sometimes."

Marjorie looks at him.

"She comes back, though," Wayne says.

Marjorie goes to speak, but stops herself. Walks towards her house and pauses at the lip of her driveway. "No need to walk me to the door, Wayne Pumphrey."

Wayne peers towards the front window and sees fingers parting the drapes, then a sliver of forehead. Half an eye. He looks back at Marjorie. She shouts in the direction of the window. "You can let go of the drapes now, Mom! *God!*"

The fingers disappear and the curtains flutter, then go still.

"Wish *she'd* pack a suitcase," Marjorie says.

Quiet for a while. Then the faint sound of a train's whistle. After it's gone, Marjorie says, "Ever wish you could hop on it?"

"Hmm?"

"The train? Ever wish you could hop on it and get the hell outta here?"

Wayne looks past her shoulder as if the train might be right behind her, then focuses back on Marjorie. "No, but I've imagined other ways."

"Oh yeah?"

"A hang glider or a hot air balloon or something. Once I had a dream that I could fly, so I flew to a place with sand and a beach and palm trees and the bluest ocean I had ever seen. I was tanned and taller and said just the right things and everyone seemed happy spending time with me. Then I woke up and my sister, Wanda, was there and I thought I might claw her eyes out."

Marjorie nods and goes to say something but decides not to. Her mother's in the window again, except more of her: a shoulder, a whole eye, some nose, mouth ... ear. Marjorie turns back to Wayne. "Go on home now."

"Okay. See you tomorrow." He starts to go, but her voice stops him.

"She used to take care of Dad but now she can't take care of herself so what am *I* supposed to do?"

Wayne doesn't know what to say.

It starts to snow.

"Never mind ... just thinking out loud. Go home."

Wayne stays where he is.

"Go home, I said."

Wayne turns around and walks down the street

and when he's in his own driveway he looks back and Marjorie's still standing where he left her and the streetlight's making her glow but he doesn't dare gawk because that's all anyone around here is good for.

# TWELVE

His father is sitting at the kitchen table holding a bag of frozen corn against his face when Wayne walks in. He points at the cast-iron frying pan near his feet and says, "Struck me with it, she did."

Footsteps in the hall. A door opening and then slamming.

"She's packing her bags," his father says. "What's new?"

Wayne notices the nearly seared-shut eyes and drooping brows and the way he's listing, as if aboard a boat. His dad takes the corn away, exposing a huge welt. Moans while working his jaw. Puts the bag back. "Two Jesus beer and this is what I get."

The sound of music, then Wanda appears, her iPod stuck in the waist of her track pants. Christina Aguilera sings something about being beautiful no matter what they say while Wanda goes to the fridge and grabs a Diet Coke and pulls back the tab and swigs. Scrunches up her face because the pop's burning and then says, "She might actually get out the door this time."

His dad grunts. "And go where?"

No one says anything.

"She's got nowhere."

A door suddenly opens, followed by: "Son of a bitch!" The same door slams.

"Am I?" his father shouts. "That what I am— *ouch!*" He holds his cheek for a moment and then says, "Who hit who, for Jesus' sake?" He looks at Wayne and Wanda. "Could have blinded me."

His mother's voice again. Muffled. Must be in the closet yanking clothes from hangers, Wayne thinks. "Youngsters!" she says. "Come here so I can talk to you!"

"Go on," his father says. "See what the loony wants."

Wayne goes to his parents' bedroom and opens the door and sticks his head in. His mother is sitting in the middle of the floor with her face in her hands. A filled suitcase lies open on the bed. She lifts her head. "Where is he?"

"Sitting at the table."

"Should have hit him harder. Drunk bastard." She wipes her eyes. "Coming with me?"

Wayne steps into the room. "Where?"

"Anywhere that's not here."

Wanda comes in and sits down on the bed and says, "His cheek's purple," then takes a sip of her Coke.

"Hope he dies."

"*Mom*."

"Well what's he good for, Wanda?"

Wanda doesn't say.

"Always taking his side, you are." Their mother gets up and goes over to the bed and zips up the suitcase and grips the handle and lifts and says, "You two coming?"

Silence.

"Or you can stay with Him and what kind of life will that be?"

Wanda looks over at Wayne, then back at their mother. "But you'll come back."

"No—"

"We'll pack and then you'll change your mind—"

"Not this time. This is for real."

Silence.

The sound of something breaking, then his dad's faraway voice: "Two Jesus beer!" and "Could have blinded me!"

"I oughtta stay," Wanda says then. "So he doesn't burn down the house."

"Suit yourself," his mother says. She looks at Wayne.

He thinks of his notebooks filled with letters underneath clothes in his dresser, beneath his mattress, stuffed in boxes on the top shelf of his closet. How long to pack them all? he wonders. What about his clothes and books and whatever else he might need? Besides, Wanda's right: she'll come back. She always does.

His mother turns and leaves the room and walks down the hall towards the kitchen and Wayne follows and considers the possibility that, this time, she *won't* come back, so who'll make the dumplings and molasses tarts and sweeten his tea just the way he likes it and make sure her husband brings home his cheque and that Wanda doesn't listen to Nickelback at the table or drink more than three Diet Cokes a day and tell him he's handsome and that, one day, he'll have more friends than he'll know what to do with?

Now his mother's in the kitchen and Wanda and he are beside her and she stops in front of their dad and says, "I need a ride."

His father takes the corn away, his cheek swollen to twice its normal size. "See what you did?" He squeezes his eyes from the pain and when he opens them they're wet.

"Did you hear me?" she says.

"A ride? I can barely see out of my Jesus eye."

"Just need a foot and a hand to drive," their mother says. "Or I'll call a cab—

"Wayne, call me a taxi." She turns back to her husband. "What? What's so goddamned funny?"

"Nothing. Wayne, put 'Working Man' on for your mom—"

"No, you drunk bastard."

"Drunk?"

"Rita MacNeil is not going to fix it this time."

"Two Jesus beer—"

"I'll never set foot in this house again—"

"I'm more sober than you are."

"More sober than I am—just listen to him, youngsters—"

"No call to hit me in the face—"

"Shoulda aimed for the temple—"

"Why didn't ya—"

"Don't know—the frying pan is heavy."

Silence all of a sudden.

His dad sets the corn on the table and then runs his fingers over his cheek as one would over a smooth stone while his mom goes into the foyer (followed by Wayne) and gets into her coat and boots. Wanda grabs another Diet Coke and then goes into the foyer, too.

Finally, his father says, "Come back in, Ruth."

"Frig off, you. I'm heading to the train station now, aren't I?"

"No trains tonight."

"Then I'll go to Dot's and leave in the morning."

His dad curses. "I'm sure that's just what Dot and Frank want—you barging in with a packed suitcase and a snotty nose. They've got little ones, Ruth."

"Dot and me are friends."

"Not for long, if you go over there."

His mother hesitates for a moment, then zips up her coat and says to Wayne, "Did you call a taxi?"

Wayne goes to do it, but his mother's voice stops him. "No, never mind, I'll walk. Walk'll do me good."

"It's freezing," says his father.

"No one's talking to you," his mom says. She ties her laces and picks up her suitcase and gives Wayne and Wanda a look and says, "I'm fed up," then pushes open the door and leaves.

No one says anything.

Wayne goes over and stands on his tiptoes and watches her through the window in the door. She's standing in the middle of the street looking up and then down the road. She starts off in one direction, but then changes course and goes the other way. Then she stops again and sets down her suitcase and puts her hands in her pockets.

"What's she doing?" Wanda says.

"She coming back?" says his father.

Wayne doesn't answer either question, just watches his mother take her hands out of her pockets and wipe her nose and pick her suitcase back up and then start walking again, except faster, the top of her leaning forward as if through a gale. After a moment there's no sight of her, so Wayne turns away from the window and sees that Wanda has gone and his father is trying to light a cigarette.

"Better make this quick before she comes back," his dad says. He puts the Zippo to his ear and shakes it and tries again but it still won't light, so he takes the smoke out of his mouth and places it behind his ear, then leans against the wall to stay upright. After a while, he says, "She'll be back."

Wayne nods.

His father makes to go, then stops. "There's supper in the oven. Fish sticks and French fries. Supposed to have corn, but I used it on my face."

Wayne nods again.

His dad gets as far as the kitchen when Wayne's voice stops him.

"What?" his father says.

"I said maybe you ought to cut back."

"Cut back?"

"Mom mightn't pack so much then."

His father doesn't speak for ages. Then, at last, he says, "Tomorrow. I'll cut back tomorrow." He turns and leaves and Wayne goes back to looking out the window in the door and soon hears something

drop in the kitchen, followed by curses and then
something else dropping and then silence.

———

Dear Dad,
     Even though you probably deserved that bruise
I can't help but blame Mom. And when you knock
over the garbage can when you're trying to park the
car I blame the bartender at Herb's Hideaway who
never seems to KNOW when you've had ENOUGH.
When you throw an ornament and it smashes I blame
whoever made the stupid thing in the first place, it
breaking as easy as that. When you call in sick for
work I blame the iron ore company for those awful
twelve-hour shifts and when your curses filter into the
street I blame the house for its thin walls and when
you're holding on to the toilet I blame the leftovers that
must have gone bad and when you lie and say you
didn't touch a Jesus drop I blame Mom for not believing
you and when you miss your seat I blame the chair
and when you can't get in because it's late and you've
lost your keys I blame the chain they're attached to
and when you can't remember where you put that
twenty dollars I blame Wanda because she's always
rooting around for money and when you're staring out
the window and shaking your head I blame the rain

and when you're sick to death of walking in the bloody
door I blame all of us for being here and when you
and me are silent at the breakfast table I blame myself
for not having anything to say.

Your son who blames everyone but you,
Wayne Pumphrey

# THIRTEEN

Wayne lifts his head and sees his mother standing there. He wipes the corner of his mouth and closes his notebook and looks at the clock on the kitchen wall.

His mom puts her suitcase down and sits beside him. Covers his hand with one of her freezing ones. "You should be in bed."

Wayne rubs an eye.

"Where's your father?"

"Asleep on the chesterfield."

"Passed out, you mean."

He stays quiet while his mother takes off her coat and drapes it on the back of her chair. "You eat supper?" she says.

"Mm-hm."

She gets up and fills the kettle and places it on

the burner, then leans back against the counter. Crosses her arms.

"You back for good?" he says.

It takes her so long to answer that Wayne thinks she didn't hear the question, but finally she says, "Who'd cook for your father? Dead in a week, he'd be. What?"

"Nothing. Thought you were gone for good."

She uncrosses her arms and looks like she might go over to him, but she stays where she is. "How can I leave *you*? Wanda too, but especially you because when I look at you I see me." She pauses. "What'd he say after I left?"

"Not much. Rocked in the rocking chair, then went over to the chesterfield and fell asleep."

His mother reaches up into the cupboard and takes down two mugs. Drops tea bags in. "Besides, I can't very well up and leave my Woolworths job, can I? People depend on me and the place is always packed and Jerry, the cook, says it's because I'm good with the customers. Sure, just the other day I had a man say I was the prettiest thing he ever met and what a shame it was that I was married and who was the lucky devil?" She pauses. "Don't tell your father."

It's quiet for ages, then the kettle whistles.

His mom prepares the tea and brings it over.

Wayne blows and takes a sip.

"Too sweet?" his mother says.

He shakes his head. "Perfect."

They drink and say nothing. Finally his mother goes, "Should be more like Wanda. The world could blow up and she wouldn't care."

Mumbling from the living room then. They listen. It goes quiet again. His mom says, "Even in his sleep he's got to have the last word."

They just sit there.

The fridge kicks in.

The grandfather clock chimes.

"You sick of us fighting?"

Wayne gazes into his mug. "I don't know."

She slides forward, her face close to his. Green green eyes and she smells like Juicy Fruit. She goes to speak but stops herself, then tries again. "He's an alcoholic."

Wayne holds her stare.

"You know what that is, I suppose?"

He nods.

She sits back. Rests her hands in her lap. Looks past his shoulder and, for a moment, appears lost.

Wayne lets the word settle. *Alcoholic.* He thinks about needing things—his notebooks and his Razor Point extra-fine pens and his alone time— wondering if that might make *him* an alcoholic, too.

"We'll always come second to him," his mother says.

Wayne takes his final gulp and pushes his mug aside and figures that second isn't so bad. In a race that's a silver medal. If you're the second chosen in street hockey that means you're nearly the most sought-after player. In a play, second best might mean being relegated to a supporting role. No shame in that though. Supporting characters often steal the show. People notice seconds. And thirds. Fourths even. Wayne would be happy being fifth or sixth. No, there's nothing wrong with second. Even if what's first is a bottle of Bacardi Dark.

"At least there's always food on the table," his mom says. "Hot water. And you've got plenty to wear. Wanda's always got the latest gadget."

Wayne thinks of Marjorie's sneakers. Her hands without mittens.

"Certainly couldn't survive on my Woolworths salary." She finishes off her tea and says, "Are you coming by after school tomorrow for your free fries and gravy and Pepsi in the tall glass you like?"

Wayne nods. Gets up and takes their mugs to the sink.

His mom says, "Thanks for waiting up."

Wayne looks at her, then away.

"Your father certainly wouldn't do it. Not unless I had a case of Canadian tucked under my arm. Scraping at the door like a dog then."

Wayne dries the mugs and puts them away. Folds

the drying towel and hangs it over the oven door handle.

"Wish you'd rub off on your father."

Wayne yawns.

"Go to bed. You won't be fit tomorrow."

He turns to go.

"No kiss or what?"

He goes over and kisses her cheek and when he starts to pull away she grabs him and holds on and her hair smells like the outdoors and her breath's hot on his neck and she says, "Don't ever drink."

"Okay."

"Promise."

"I promise."

She lets him go and it occurs to Wayne how tightly she's been holding him. "Go on," she says, "you'll never wake up."

Wayne lingers a moment longer, then goes.

———

Dear Mom,

I can't imagine what things would be like with just Wanda and Dad and me. We'd probably live on hot dogs and Kraft Dinner and the laundry would never get done and Wanda would drink even more Diet Coke and Dad wouldn't stop drinking PERIOD. Then he'd lose his job and the heat and lights would get cut

and someone would board up the windows and throw
us out and we'd have to find an apartment on Fallow
Crescent with the welfare crowd and the too-loud music
and the fistfights and the crying babies and the cop
cars, but seeing as you're back I guess there's no need
to worry, although what happens if someday your
leaving sticks? I'll be like Marjorie then, except it'll be
you and not Dad.

Why'd you marry him anyway? He's always been
a drinker, you've said, so did it not bother you before?
I always thought people got more used to things over
time. But maybe that's only true with certain things ...
snoring or peeing on the toilet seat or chewing with
your mouth full. Perhaps drinking and cursing and
breaking perfectly good ornaments are another matter.

Can you catch being an alcoholic? Is it in the genes
like say ... cancer or heart disease? And if so, would I
get hooked after only one sip and forget to bring home
the butter and start banging into things? Would you
have to hit ME with the frying pan, too?

It's hard when you go. Wanda acts like she couldn't
care less but I know she does because she needs
another girl to even things out. And Dad cares, too.
You should hear some of what he says when he thinks
no one is listening. Sometimes he sings that Irish song,
you know the one, and it makes me wonder why
that poor lassie pines away for her lover that never
comes back and then she's old, so it's too late anyway.

Sometimes he forgets the words and starts over. Other times he'll fall asleep in the middle of a verse and drop his tumbler.

Is it hard to see love through all the fighting?

Your son who wonders if it's hard to see love through all the fighting,
Wayne Pumphrey

# FEBRUARY

As If It Couldn't Get Any Worse

# ONE

Wayne's running, but he's not going nearly fast enough. It's the big boots, he guesses, and the soft snow, the knapsack filled with books. Harvey's laugh is in his ears. Kenny's snowballs are striking his legs and back. Pete The Meat's chanting: "You're dead Wayne Pumphrey, you're dead Wayne Pumphrey, you're dead Wayne Pumphrey …"

Where's Bobby? No sign of Bobby.

Wayne fakes left, but goes right.

"Sneaky fucker!" Harvey says.

"We got 'em!" Kenny says.

Pete The Meat goes, "You're dead Wayne Pumphrey, you're dead Wayne Pumphrey …"

Suddenly Bobby juts out between two houses and tackles him. Wayne lands hard on his back, biology and math digging into his lungs. No air. Bobby's on top of him, grinning, saliva pooling and

then dangling from his lips. Wayne turns his face just
as the spit lands on his right cheek. Twists his head
to the other side and wipes the mess off in the snow.

Bobby bears all his weight down. Presses his face
so close to Wayne's they're touching noses. "You
owe me a tooth, faggot." Bobby grabs Wayne's chin
and says, "Open up."

Wayne squeezes his mouth shut.

Pete The Meat appears then, staring down at
him. "Thought you could fool us by taking a different
route, eh, Pumphrey?"

"He thinks we're idiots," Bobby says.

Kenny's there now too, hardening a snowball.
Harvey comes and stands beside Kenny and says to
Pete, "He does, thinks he's smarter than us."

"Does he now?" The Meat says. Then to Bobby,
"Get off him."

"Just a minute longer, Pete," Bobby says.

"Get off, I said!"

Bobby does, then takes his place alongside the
others. "Fucker owes me a tooth."

"Fuckin' rights," Kenny says.

Wayne sits up.

Pete The Meat leers down at him. Arms folded.
No mitts. Knuckles the size of scallops. "Take all the
back trails you want, Pumphrey. There's no place I
can't find you."

Wayne goes to stand, but Pete knocks him back

down with the toe of his boot. Laughs. "You're weaker than a girl, Pumphrey. I almost feel bad."

"Kick him in the face, Pete," Bobby says.

Pete shakes his head. "Naw, no kicking. He's going to get what was meant for him the other day." The Meat turns to Kenny. "You ready?"

Kenny holds up his snowball. "Fuckin' rights."

"Hold 'em steady," Pete says to Harvey and Bobby. Both boys go over and stand Wayne up and grab his arms.

Kenny finds a spot no more than six feet away. Digs in his heels. Rounds the snowball despite its being round already. Gives a look to Pete.

The Meat unfolds his arms. "Hold still, Pumphrey, this won't take a minute."

Wayne looks off in the distance. Not a soul.

Pete says, "Girlfriend's not coming this time, Pumphrey. Got tied up at the butcher."

Kenny laughs, but no one else seems to get the joke. Then Wayne says, "It's her body now, isn't it? What's it to any of you what she does with it!"

No one moves.

A kind of quiet then that reminds Wayne of early morning when it's still dark and everyone is sleeping and his dad is pacing the driveway waiting for the company bus to take him to the mine and how can his father live in a full house yet look like the loneliest man on earth?

A finger is jabbing into his chest. Pete's finger, although it feels more like the tip of a screwdriver. And The Meat's smiling and nodding his head and saying, "I get it now, Pumphrey." He looks back at the others. "Get it, boys?"

Kenny keeps hardening his snowball and Harvey shrugs and Bobby says, "Get what, Pete?"

The Meat shakes his head. "Pumphrey finally got his dicky bird wet, idiot."

Kenny laughs and Harvey groans and Bobby sticks his own finger down his throat to hide his envy.

The Meat breathes StarKist on Wayne and says, "What's she like, Pumphrey?"

Wayne says nothing.

"Stuck it in the wrong hole, I bet," says Kenny.

"Either that or he blew his wad before he could get it in," goes The Meat.

Bobby says, "Probably did it in his shorts, eh, Pete?"

The Meat nods. "That what happened, Pumphrey? You jizz in your sister's panties—"

*"Fuck off!"*

Who said that? Harvey? Kenny? Probably Kenny. Although it could have been The Meat. The first word Pete learned probably, Wayne thinks, before *jail* and *punch*. Why is everyone staring? Does Bobby's mouth usually hang open wide enough to see the cavities in his back molars? And The Meat's

face ... it's never *that* red, is it? Kenny has just
dropped his snowball and is not bothering to pick
it back up. What's Harvey saying: something about
being dead because no one tells The Meat to fuck
off and lives. Now Bobby's repeating what Harvey
has just said and it suddenly occurs to Wayne that
it was he himself who said it and he wonders how a
person can say something without thinking about it.
Then The Meat comes forward and he's got his arms
raised like he's ready to fight and Wayne shuts his
eyes because it's better not to look sometimes and
that's when he feels the warmth in his shorts, which
runs down his leg and into one sock, one boot. He
opens his eyes and sees that Pete has already noticed,
followed by Kenny, Harvey, and Bobby at pretty
much the same time.

The loudest laughter that Wayne thinks he's ever
heard then. The gut-holding and stomping feet kind,
and then they're letting Wayne go because they can't
breathe. Bobby actually falls to his knees; Harvey
bends over and holds his thighs; The Meat, unchar-
acteristically, jumps on the spot.

And Wayne runs. His boots might have slowed
him earlier, but not now, no. He's like the wind
now, Flash Gordon, a cheetah, his feet aren't even
touching the ground. No sound, not even their
laughter. Pants hardening from the piss. Is it possible
to run forever? he wonders. He'll try.

# TWO

Wayne's naked from the waist down and throwing his pants and underwear into the clothes hamper when the bathroom door suddenly opens. "I'm in here!" he shouts.

"Jesus!" his father says, closing the door. "What are you doing home?"

"Nothing."

"Aren't you supposed to be at school—What? I can't hear you."

"I said I don't want to go today."

"Why not?"

No answer.

"*Wayne?*"

"Aren't *you* supposed to be at work?"

"Hey, we're talking about *you* now."

No sound from Wayne's side of the door.

"Come out," his father says.

"I'm not done—"

"Out, I said. I need to use it."

"I'm not wearing pants."

"Grab a towel. Hurry up."

A moment later Wayne comes out, a beige towel wrapped around his waist.

"What the hell were you doing in there?" his dad says, pushing past him.

Wayne runs to his bedroom and slams the door and puts on clean underwear and brown cords and sits on the edge of his bed with a palm over each knee. He stares at the wall and imagines himself passing through it into another place but even there The Meat's pointing and breathing tuna and smoothing his almost-a-moustache and Wayne wonders if there's anywhere that Pete isn't.

Knocking on his door, then the knob turning and catching. His father's voice: "Since when do you lock your door?"

Wayne stays quiet.

"Wayne!"

"I'm sick."

"Sick?"

"I threw up."

"Did you?"

"On my way to school."

Silence.

His father coughs, then says, "Let me in."

"I just want to lie down—"

"I'll put a bucket by your bed—"

"If I could just sleep—"

"Give you a Gravol—"

"If I need anything, I'll sing out."

Nothing for a moment, followed by the sound of his father resting his weight against the door. After a while, he says, "I called in sick." Then, "Wayne?"

"I heard you."

"Don't tell your mother."

Silence.

"Wayne?"

"Okay."

"All right then. Go to sleep. I'll be in the living room if you need me."

Wayne waits until his father pushes himself away from the door and walks down the hall before getting up and going over to sit at his desk. He opens a nearly filled notebook and grabs a Razor Point extra-fine pen and writes:

Dear Pete The Meat,

Is it the way I walk? Talk? Is it because I'm small? Is my laugh strange? My voice? Do I smell funny or dress stupid or style my hair the wrong way? Are my eyes too far apart? WHAT? Or maybe I'm ~~juts~~ just an easy target, slow and easy to grab hold of and to give

a wedgie to, is that it? Do I remind you of someone
you hate? Is it because I sometimes piss my pants and
this is something for you and Bobby and Harvey and
Kenny to laugh about and point fingers at and then
get other people's attention so that they can laugh
and point too? Am I a joke? Am I like a wrestling mat:
something for you to lie and sweat and bleed on? Is it
because I'm weak? Because I like drama and writing,
but I also like UFC, did you know? Is it because your
dad's not your real one and that you had a tough
start but lots of kids live with people that aren't their
biological parents and they turn out fine. Is it because
you're afraid of me? I don't mean in the physical sense,
but is there something about me you fear? Is that what
this is about? Do you think it doesn't bother me? That
I can get up and walk away and just forget about it?
Do you think my pissy clothes wash themselves? Do
you think I like eating yellow snow and being tackled
by Bobby and having to smell tuna on your breath?
Maybe I hate you too, even more than you hate me
and maybe someday I'll wait outside your door and
when you open it I'll shoot you in the head and then
you'll be sorry, won't you? How would you like that?
I just wish you'd leave me alone ~~becasue~~ because
I'm tired and I'm only fifteen so I shouldn't be, right?
I've been searching for a reason, you see, and I can't
find one and I've come to believe that things don't just
happen. So if there's something I've done let me know

and I'll stop doing it 'cause I just want to get these three years over with so I can get out of here.

The one you pick on that would like to know the reason,
Wayne Pumphrey

—

Wayne opens his eyes and sees his father sitting there: checkered shirt and brown slacks and hair actually combed and slicked back like Tony Soprano and his cheek's so swollen it looks like he's stuffed grapes in his mouth and he's playing with his Zippo lighter. He looks at Wayne and says, "You're awake."

Wayne nods and thinks he was a youngster the last time his father sat on the edge of his bed like this: a tugged toe, a hand messing his hair, a prickly kiss on his forehead. "What time is it?"

His dad glances at his watch. "Ten-thirty. How's your stomach?"

"Gurgling," Wayne says. "Might need to sleep all day. How'd you get in?"

His father flips open and then closes the lid of his Zippo. "That lock's useless."

Wayne looks at his father's face and says, "Your cheek broken?"

"Naw. Sore as Jesus, though." His dad focuses on the space between his feet and says, "What's the real reason you're not in school?"

Wayne lies back down and pulls the sheets up. The silence presses down on him and makes it hard to breathe and he thinks it's even worse than having toothless Bobby on top.

"Got the strangest call a few minutes ago," his father says at last. "Turns out Donna Hiscock was staring out her back window this morning and what do you think she saw?"

Wayne turns over on his side and tucks his knees into his chest and closes his eyes and hears the lighter flicking open again, then closing ... opening ... closing.

"A bunch of boys is what ... picking on another boy. A smaller boy."

Wayne imagines giant hands coming through the ceiling and plucking him from his bed and covering him and carrying him somewhere where there's no Zippo lighter and no father with a swollen cheek and no piss-soaked pants in the hamper down the hall ...

"Now she couldn't be absolutely sure—her eyes being what they are—but she could have sworn that the tiny boy belonged to the sweet woman named Ruth that she used to work with at Woolworths."

... and no iron ore mine and no eight months

of winter and no band called Nickelback and no
mother swinging a heavy frying pan and no girl up
the road with a dead father and a mother who may
as well be ...

"She would have called sooner, but it took her
a while to find your mother's number. Would have
grabbed a broom and gone outside herself, she said,
if not for being seventy-odd."

... and no old ladies staring out of windows
and soggy turkey sandwiches and cancer-causing
Crunchits and small bladders and snotty noses and
tears and places to always have to fit into—

"Wayne?"

"What?"

"Why were you throwing your pants in the
hamper?"

Silence.

A hand gripping his ankle and squeezing and his
father saying, "Who were they?"

"That lady's blind."

"Turn around, Wayne."

"Let me sleep."

"I said turn *around*— Ouch!" His dad covers his
cheek. "Don't make me yell."

Wayne turns, finds a place beyond his father's
shoulder to set his eyes.

His father rests his elbows on his knees. Interlaces
his fingers. When he speaks again his voice is calmer.

"A scuffle every now and then is to be expected. But what happened to you is something else."

A long silence.

"They hurt you?" his dad says.

"No."

"Speak up."

"No, I said."

Wayne looks away from the wall and down at his father's hands and notices blood pooling at their fingertips. His father says, "How long's it been going on?"

Wayne shrugs.

"Give me names."

Wayne won't.

"You're not a tattle and that's good, but sometimes it isn't, so tell me who they are or would you rather I went to the school myself?"

"No, don't!"

"Then tell me."

Wayne goes to speak, but doesn't, so his father gets up and goes to the door and grips the knob and says over his shoulder, "Drive on over now, perhaps—"

"Pete The Meat."

His dad turns around. "What?"

"Pete The Meat."

"What kinda name is that?"

"It's because he's got veins in his biceps and can

make his chest muscles move without touching them."

His father pauses. "He have a last name?"

"Moved here three years ago and he had a tough start and has a second father and he struck a teacher once."

"*Wayne.*"

"Avery. His last name's Avery."

"Okay. Who else?"

"No one."

"*Who?* I said."

"Harvey and Bobby and Kenny, but they only do it 'cause Pete makes them."

His father goes quiet for a moment, then says, "Where's he live, this Pete The Meat?"

"Why do you want to know?"

"Just answer me."

"I don't know and I wish now I never told you anything."

"Get up."

"What?"

"You're no sicker than I am and I think we'll pay Pete's parents a visit."

"*No!*"

"Or we'll go see the principal. Your choice."

"You'll make it worse."

"Let's go."

"His parents are working."

"I'll take my chances."

"I don't know where he lives, I already told you."

"I think you do, Wayne. Now get your jacket."

"No."

*"Wayne!"*

"I'm weak like a girl already!"

"What—"

"And I eat yellow snow and if you go to Pete's I'll be the one who needs his dad to fight his battles *too,* and I've always come second to you before so why can't we just keep it that way!"

His dad opens his mouth to say something but nothing comes out and he tries to leave but can't seem to get the door open, so he faces Wayne instead and for the longest time doesn't speak, but then finally he says, "No point crying."

Wayne wipes his eyes. "I'm not." For a moment he thinks his father might come over and sit on the bed again, but his dad steps back instead, letting the door take his weight, and puts his hands in his pockets and stares down at his wool socks. After a while he goes, "Your Uncle Philip was small too."

Wayne fiddles with the comforter.

"In school he could make up a joke on the spot and deliver it like a stand-up comic and he'd have the bullies laughing so hard they'd forget why they were picking on him."

Wayne sets his eyes on his father's.

"So I never had to worry. But *you* ... I don't know, you're different ... softer. What are you supposed to do if you can't fight back or say something funny, so we'll go and talk to this Pete's parents and no one else has to know."

Wayne turns away and imagines those giant hands again and this time they're taking him to a place where fathers don't make bad situations worse and where small and weak and soft are things to be admired, then he turns and looks up and notices his door is half open and his father is gone, so he lies back and dreams of another half-open door and slipping through it like a phantom, away from everything.

# THREE

His father pulls into Pete The Meat's driveway and
shuts off the engine. Looks over at Wayne and says,
"You ready?"

Wayne nods and goes to grip the door handle
but then changes his mind. "They say his second
father owns a shotgun and that he spends all his time
polishing it and pointing it and firing it like it's some
joke."

"Wayne—"

"And that he's got a tattoo of a tear beneath his
left eye."

"What foolishness—"

"And his mother spends hours each day over a
huge pot of pork and chicken and she just plunks it
down and Pete and his second father reach in with
their bare hands and tear the flesh from the bones
like wolves and then they even eat the bones—"

"Wayne—"

"And grease is all over their faces and it drips on their clothes and then Mrs. Avery puts the pot back on the stove and starts all over again and she's exhausted—"

"That's enough."

"I'm just telling you what I heard."

"Come on."

They get out of the car and walk along the driveway and up the porch stairs and his dad rings the bell, and Wayne imagines the barrel of the gun, then the trigger, and the thick finger pressing against it followed by the arm and shoulder and neck and finally the pale, angry face of Mr. Avery: the little slit of a mouth and a Hitler moustache, probably, and that tear tattoo beneath cold, dead eyes—

A woman's suddenly standing in the doorway and she's nothing like the worn, drawn-out wife and mother he was expecting, and she's wearing a grey cardigan and jeans with holes in the knees and eyeliner and her teeth are perfect.

"Mrs. Avery?" his father says.

She nods. "Yes."

"I'm Calvin Pumphrey and this here's Wayne. He goes to school with your boy, Pete."

She takes in his father's cheek. "Peter, yes."

His dad touches his bruise like he's just as surprised as Pete's mother to find it there. "You wouldn't say it by looking at him, but Wayne's got a hell of a slapshot."

Mrs. Avery tries smiling while his father says how sorry he is to have shown up unannounced and holds out his hand and what choice does Pete's mom have but to shake it?

Wayne holds out his hand too and Mrs. Avery grabs it and her grip is soft and warm like fresh bread and she says, "Weren't you one of the wise men in the pageant last year?"

"I brought frankincense."

"You tripped."

"Costume was too big."

"Upset the manger," his father says.

Mrs. Avery puts her hands in the pockets of her cardigan because she must be cold with the door open, and says, "Stole the show."

Another voice then, a man's. "Who is it, Maureen?"

"Mr. Pumphrey and his son, Wayne," she says over her shoulder.

"Who?"

"Come see for yourself."

Wayne imagines two cartridges being loaded into the chamber, then Mr. Avery's grin, his quick steps up the basement stairs. Bury them in the basement, most likely.

Suddenly Pete's new dad is standing there and

he's shorter than his wife and smaller boned; he's wearing a V-neck sweater and slippers and he's clean-shaven. "Hello," he says.

Wayne can't find any tear tattoo.

More handshakes and his dad explains the bruise again and then he and his father are invited in and led to a room off the kitchen where there are floor-to-ceiling windows and a crackling fire and a bearskin rug. Wayne sits on a leather sofa with his father while Mr. Avery settles into an armchair and Mrs. Avery wonders out loud why she's neglected to offer them tea and something to eat.

"Don't go to any trouble," his dad says, but Mrs. Avery flicks her wrist and is gone.

Quiet for a moment, then Mr. Avery looks at Wayne and says, "No school today?"

Wayne shakes his head and imagines popping in the fire like an ember.

His father clears his throat and sits forward and says: "That's why we're here."

"Oh?"

"No sense in beating around the bush, is there?"

Mr. Avery grips the arms of his chair like a nervous flier.

"Apparently your boy's been giving mine a hard time and you can see how small he is, so it's a bit unfair."

Mr. Avery looks over but doesn't say anything.

His father says, "Tell him, Wayne."

Wayne's just about to, but then Mrs. Avery walks back in carrying a plate of sweets, which she sets down on the coffee table in front of him and his father before making her way back over to her husband. Pete's second dad moves his hand and she sits on the arm of the chair and says, "It'll be a few minutes for the tea."

"Thank you," his father says, grabbing a snowball. He looks at Wayne. "Say thank you."

Wayne does, then takes a Rice Krispie square and sets it on his lap and what time is it—does anyone know? Couldn't The Meat walk in at any minute?

His dad's trying to swallow what's in his mouth and talk at the same time and what he's saying is: "Donna Hiscock was staring out her window this morning and saw a bunch of boys picking on Wayne here and one of them, the ringleader, was your boy, Pete—Peter, excuse me."

"Who was staring out their window?" Mr. Avery says, followed by Pete's mom saying, "*Our* Peter?" and then Mr. Avery going, "Did you say ringleader?"

"That's what Wayne told me."

The Meat's parents exchange glances and then Mr. Avery says, "You're sure about this?"

"What did Peter *do*?" The Meat's mom says.

"He's very sure. Aren't you, Wayne?"

Wayne imagines the looks from the girls

standing beside the water fountain when word gets out. The boys, too: smoking and pointing and flicking their lit cigarettes and calling him "rat," and he can already feel the weight of Pete and Harvey and Bobby and Kenny as he's being pinned face first into the snow. *Now hump it, Pumphrey. Thatta boy. Faster.*

"*Wayne?*" his father says.

Wayne looks up with a start and his Rice Krispie square falls on the floor, so he picks it up and blows on it and puts it back on his lap and says that, Yes, he's sure, then an ember shoots out of the fire and lands on the hardwood and Mr. Avery gets up and stomps on it as if it might burn the house down and then he goes over and grabs a poker and stokes the flames despite there already being enough heat to melt the skin off their faces.

Mrs. Avery says, "Would someone *please* tell me what's going on?"

Pete's second father turns around to face his wife, the poker still in his hand, making Wayne wonder if the V-neck sweater and slippers and neat haircut are all a front for what he *really* has in mind ... to bludgeon them to death with the smouldering poker.

"Peter's been bullying Wayne," Mr. Avery says.

Pete's mom looks over at Wayne and his father like she doesn't remember having invited them in, then sort of laughs and says, "There must be some mistake."

Mr. Avery finally puts the poker down and goes back over to the chair, but he doesn't sit, preferring instead to rest a hand on his wife's shoulder. He looks at Wayne and says, "How long's it been going on?"

"This doesn't make any sense," Mrs. Avery says. "He's been so good," to which her husband replies, "There now, Maureen, there now."

"Tell them, Wayne," his dad says.

Pete's mom looks on the verge of tears, then the kettle starts whistling and Mr. Avery wonders if she wouldn't mind going and making the tea and taking the young one with her because he needs to have a private word with Mr. Pumphrey and not to worry because he'll fill her in on everything later.

Pete's mom heads off, and Wayne's father squeezes his thigh and tells him to go too, so Wayne follows her into the kitchen and stands beside the table, gripping the back of a chair.

"Sit," she tells him.

He does.

She makes tea and sets everything on a wooden tray and leaves, then comes back and puts what's left in front of Wayne and says, "Don't be shy."

Wayne takes a cup and adds milk and sugar and stirs and then rests the spoon beside his Rice Krispie square.

"Peter would eat the whole tray if I let him," Mrs. Avery says.

Wayne takes a bite and strains to hear the words coming from the other room and they're mostly jumbled, but a few he makes out: *youngster, neglected, resentment, fresh start—*"

The Meat's mom is saying something.

"Sorry?" he says.

"What's he done? I asked."

Wayne takes another bite and imagines The Meat walking in and seeing him there. A lot worse than eating yellow snow then, he bets.

Another word seeps into the kitchen. *Therapist.* Then another. *Happier.*

"I'd hate to get him in trouble," Wayne says.

"Don't worry about that."

"It was nothing at first," Wayne says at last. "Some name-calling. Drawings taped to my locker."

"Drawings?"

"Some were funny ... others not so much— What time will he be home because sometimes the cafeteria food's so bad no one will stick around."

"He rarely comes home for lunch. If *cardboard* was on the menu, he'd eat it."

Silence.

"Go on, Wayne. Don't be afraid."

He picks a Rice Krispie off his square and puts it in his mouth. Grips the handle of his cup. "Pushing started later. Tripping in the cafeteria. Charley horses. Snowballs whipped at me. Sometimes I'd have to eat yellow snow or lie on my stomach and ..."

"Yes, Wayne?"

"I'd rather not say."

A long time passes, then Mrs. Avery says, "You must think Peter's mean."

Wayne looks away.

She reaches out and pats the back of his hand and says she's sorry and Wayne wonders why she should be sorry because of something her son did.

More words from the other room—his father's: *weaker, writing, different.*

"Sometimes he does bad things but he's not a bad person," Pete's mom says. "I'll talk to him. He listens to me."

Wayne squeezes his cup and he goes to speak, but then stops himself.

"What?" Mrs. Avery says.

"Naw, nothing."

"Tell me."

She waits.

Finally, Wayne goes, "Everyone says that Pete had a tough start and that Mr. Avery's not his real dad and I couldn't help but wonder what happened to the first one and I hope it isn't rude to ask."

Pete's mom holds Wayne's stare for a moment, then she sits back with her arms folded across

her chest and tries to see beyond the frost on the
window. After a very long time, she says, "It's awful
the way people talk." She pauses. "Peter's real father
left and neither of us misses him."

Laughter from the other room then and a door
being pushed open and a voice shouting, "What's
for lunch?" and Wayne has to grip the table to keep
from falling off his chair.

Mr. Avery is talking and he must be shouting
because Wayne can hear every word, and what he
says is for Pete to forget about lunch and to sit his
ass down because there's something that needs
addressing and does he know who the man on the
sofa is?

Then Mrs. Avery's hand is on top of his and she's
asking Wayne if he's all right but there's no spit in
his mouth and his throat is closed over, so how can
he answer?

"It's Mr. Pumphrey," Mr. Avery says from the
other room. "His boy's Wayne."

A long silence.

"Something you want to tell me, Peter?"

Now Pete's mom is saying something to Wayne
about following her into the living room and not to
worry because soon everything will be sorted out.

Wayne and Pete are sitting side by side on the sofa. Pete's mother is in the armchair while her husband paces the floor. Wayne's dad is beside the fire, the dancing flames projecting onto one side of his face like a silent movie.

Quiet save for Mr. Avery's slippers scuffing along the hardwood, and the still-crackling fire.

Wayne focuses on his own lap.

Pete The Meat's got his arms folded across his chest.

Mr. Avery stops pacing and looks at his son and says, "We're still waiting, Peter."

Silence.

"You're upsetting your mother."

Pete's mom slides forward so that her bum is half off the chair. "Tell us, hon. Please."

More quiet. Then a log collapses on itself, sending up a cascade of sparks and embers, which no one can resist staring into. Afterwards, Pete says, "It was all meant in good fun. Didn't mean to hurt him."

"Well you *did,* Peter," Mr. Avery says. "You're twice his size for God's sake. What were you thinking?"

Pete doesn't answer.

"You owe him and his father an apology, and you'd better bloody well mean it, because your mother and I are really trying here, buddy, and you're almost a man now, so you ought to start acting like it."

Pete pauses. "I'm sorry."

"Tell *Wayne,* not me."

Wayne feels The Meat's eyes burning through his skin, exposing his insides, and he wishes he and his father could toss this day into the fire and watch it burn to ash and get into their car and just drive away.

"I'm sorry, Wayne," Pete The Meat says. "I guess me and the boys went too far."

"Good," says Mrs. Avery.

"His father, too," Mr. Avery says.

Pete turns to Wayne's dad and says, "Sorry, Mr. Pumphrey. We didn't mean to upset or scare him or anything. He's a good sport, Wayne is."

Wayne's father nods.

Pete's mom says to her husband, "Shouldn't they shake on it?"

"Yes, good idea, that's the gentlemanly thing to do." Then, "Whenever you're ready, boys."

Wayne lifts his head and looks over at Pete and sees that The Meat is already holding out his hand.

"Go on, Wayne," his dad tells him.

Wayne grips Pete's hand and it's huge, the fingers like metal, and they latch on and squeeze and if not for being in front of everyone, he'd cry out.

"Friends from now on," Mrs. Avery says, to

which her husband replies, "Yes, friends," while Pete The Meat keeps squeezing and grinning, and it suddenly dawns on Wayne what's beneath that smile, and what it is, is: *You're dead, Pumphrey ... coming to my house. Fuckin' DEAD!*

# FOUR

His father parks in front of the strip mall and shuts
off the car. Grips the steering wheel and stares
forward, then takes the keys out of the ignition
and puts them in his pocket and says to Wayne,
"Back in a minute." He opens the door and Wayne
says,

"No, you won't."

"What?"

"Be back in a minute."

His father—half of him inside the car and half
of him out—seems unsure suddenly, as if he's
forgotten what he's supposed to be doing right in
the middle of doing it. For ages his dad stays that
way and the cold's getting in and it occurs to Wayne
that staying where you are isn't always the wrong
thing, but then the car door slams shut and his father
is walking away and tucking his chin into his coat

collar because the wind has picked up since leaving Pete The Meat's.

Wayne watches him pass Mike's Convenience, a dollar store, an arcade, and Pizza Delight before coming to a stop in front of a neon sign with some of its letters burnt out. ERB'S HID AWAY it says, although Wayne knows it's HERB'S HIDEAWAY because it's the place his mother most often accuses his father of going to.

His dad puts his hands in his pockets and stares at the sign for ages, then pulls open the door and goes in.

Wayne waits and wonders why his father wouldn't have left the car running. Freeze to death in here. Can't even listen to the radio or a CD. He breathes on the window and fogs it up and writes the word *weak*, then wipes it away. Thinks then of The Meat's handshake and of his own fingers nearly breaking and the way Pete walked him and his father to the door afterwards and then stood on the porch waving until they drove away. *You're dead, Pumphrey . . . coming to my house. Fuckin' DEAD.*

The door to Herb's opens and a man comes out and he lights a cigarette and takes a few drags and walks away.

Wayne notices the E in HIDEAWAY flash on for a second, then go out again. He zips up his jacket.

One-thirty becomes two-thirty and Wayne's

freezing just sitting in the car, so he gets out and starts walking. Past Mike's Convenience, the dollar store, the arcade, and Pizza Delight, and then stopping where his father stopped. He moves to the window and presses his nose against the glass but there's too much frost to see anything. He moves to the door but doesn't go in. A woman walks past and makes some comment about how Herb's is a grown-up place and why isn't he in school anyway, and Wayne looks down at his feet and pretends not to hear. When she's gone, he lifts his head and opens the door a crack and tries to get a peek inside, but it's too dark and there's country music and the sound of a slot machine. He opens the door wider and slips in and stands in the foyer, listening to the music. The singer's singing about where he's going to live when he gets home, and how his old lady has thrown out everything he owns.

A woman shouts.

Someone curses.

He takes a few steps and looks around the corner. A man with a beer belly and wearing a ball cap is playing the slot machine while a woman with an even bigger beer belly is standing behind him. She grips his shoulder and says, "Come on, Kyle, you've played long enough."

"Leave me," Kyle says.

"Aren't we going out? You said we were."

"This *is* out."

There's no one else in the place save for Wayne's father sitting at the bar, his fist wrapped around a Bacardi Dark, and a tall bartender who's busy flicking the stations on a TV that appears to be suspended from the ceiling.

The woman says, "'Somewhere nice,' you said."

"Go home out of it, Tammy; you're bad luck."

"Cocksucker!"

"Hey!" says the bartender.

Tammy turns to the bartender and says, "Tell him to stop, Bert."

Bert rests his hands on the bar and leans across it. "He wants to spend his money on my machine, I'm not going to stop him."

"*His* money!"

"I don't care whose it is, Tammy; just keep it down, okay. I'd like a few minutes' peace before Happy Hour."

Tammy sulks and waddles off and sits at a table by herself.

His father lifts his empty glass, so Bert gets him another and plunks it down. His dad takes a long sip and wipes his mouth on his coat sleeve and then says something to Bert, which makes Bert laugh. Then Tammy's saying, "You let youngsters in here now?"

"Huh?" Bert says, looking to where Tammy's pointing.

Wayne suddenly realizes that it's him they're looking at. Then his father is staring too and Wayne thinks about going back to the car, but then his dad is asking Bert if it's all right if his boy comes in and Bert nods and says, "Come on over, young fella, so we can get a look at ya."

Wayne walks up to the bar and Tammy says, "He's awful tiny," and Bert says, "He *is* small, Calvin." Then his father reaches out and messes Wayne's hair and asks why he's not waiting in the car and Wayne says because it's freezing and his father laughs and roots around in his pocket and pulls out the keys and hands them to Wayne.

"How old's he?" Tammy says.

"Fifteen," says his father.

She laughs and says, "He looks younger."

Wayne's thankful for the gloom, because he feels his face grow hot.

Bert says, "Nothing wrong with looking young, eh, Wayne?"

Wayne nods.

"I suppose," Tammy says.

Kyle punches the slot machine and says, "Jesus Christ!"

"Kyle!" shouts Bert. "What did I tell you about hitting the machine?"

"I'm sorry, Bert, but she's not giving me an inch today."

Tammy says, "And he could sure *use* an inch, too."

"That's fine talk there, Tammy," goes Kyle. Then to Wayne's dad and Bert: "The filth that comes outta that woman's mouth."

"Let's go home, Kyle. *Please*."

"In a bloody minute. Give me a toonie."

"I won't."

"Come on, Tammy, a measly toonie's not gonna kill ya."

"No, but the thirty dollars you've already spent will. I was supposed to buy Mom a birthday gift."

"For God's sake, your mother doesn't know Osama bin Laden's dead."

"You're heartless, Kyle."

"If you give me a toonie, I'll massage your toes later."

Tammy pauses, then reaches into her purse and says to Bert and Wayne's dad, "He knows how to play me, that one." She goes over and gives Kyle the money and Kyle winks and pats her bottom and drops the coin in and starts playing. Tammy stays watching.

"Go on now, Wayne," his dad says. "I shouldn't be much longer."

"Can't you come now?"

"Not yet."

"Why?"

"Because."

"Because what?"

"*Wayne* ... go wait in the car."

Wayne turns around and starts walking and hears Bert say, "Nice to meet you," and then Kyle shouting, "Three cherries!" and then Tammy clapping.

Wayne pushes open the door and goes outside and it's colder somehow and the sun's already lower in the sky. He makes his way back to the car and sits in the driver's seat and turns the ignition and blasts the heat. He puts in a blank CD and it must be his mother's, because Rita MacNeil is singing about being a working man and living underground, so Wayne turns it off and sits there in silence. But then he puts the CD in again and turns it up and why shouldn't he listen to it? The heat or Rita's folksy voice makes Wayne drowsy, so he rests his head against the steering wheel and sleeps.

—

Wayne's choking on a Rice Krispie square as Nickelback sings that song from the first *Spider-Man* movie. Pete's second dad must be stoking the fire still, because it's so hot. Someone's on top of him and it's his father wanting to know why his son would eat yellow snow and piss his pants and run away instead of fighting. And Wayne tries to answer, but there's no voice, and then his father is laughing and drinking Bacardi Dark and some of it spills into Wayne's eyes and it burns and he cries out—

He wakes and sits back and tries to catch his breath. Wipes his mouth with the back of his hand and turns off the heat because it's like a sauna. It's dark outside. He looks at the time and it's nearly four-thirty and his mother must be getting supper ready while Wanda drinks Diet Coke and dreams of being kidnapped and taken on tour by Chad Kroeger.

Then the door opens and his father is telling him to scoot over, so Wayne climbs into the passenger side and buckles his seat belt and thinks about walking instead. But then his father is backing out and putting the car in drive and the wheels are spinning on the ice for ages until finding traction. No signal light when his father makes a left onto Marconi Street. No stopping at the stop sign farther along, either. A motorist coming in the other direction blasts her horn because she's supposed to have the right-of-way.

"Slow down," Wayne says.

His father doesn't. Takes the turn onto Glendale Street too sharply and the car fishtails and Wayne presses his palms against the dash and a light pole nearly takes out the side mirror.

*"Dad!"*

"What?"

*"You're all over the road!"*

His father eases up on the gas and pushes in the car lighter. After a while he says, "If your mother asks, Pete's father handed me a beer and what, I'm supposed to refuse a man in his own house?" He fumbles for his cigarettes. "Don't mention that I was smoking in the car, either." He frees one from the pack and jams it between his lips and then takes the left onto Willow Avenue.

In the silence, Wayne breathes in rum and wonders if it's possible to get drunk off the fumes, then the lighter pops and his father grabs it and lights his cigarette and blows a steady stream of smoke out through his nose. Cracks the window.

No words between them.

His dad puffs.

Wayne steals glances at the speedometer.

A long ash on the cigarette now, which his father tries flicking out the window, but it lands on his pants, so he curses and tries wiping it away and doesn't see the yellow light that's turning red up ahead nor the lady and her border collie, so Wayne shouts *"Dad!"* and his father looks up and brakes hard and the car slides halfway into the intersection.

*"Watch where you're going!"* screams the woman, showing her middle finger. Her dog barks and gets to its hind legs.

His father goes to back up, but there's a car waiting, so he stays where he is.

"I've got your licence plate number," says the woman.

His dad ignores her and when the light turns green he stomps on the gas like his foot's a hundred pounds and soon the woman and her dog disappear so completely into the blackness that Wayne's not sure they were there at all.

His father throws his cigarette out the window and turns onto Lakeside Drive. Then he's shaking his head and cursing under his breath and when Wayne asks, he says, "Don't ever eat yellow snow again."

Wayne looks away, out the passenger-side window. Grips the door handle because home's not far away and he longs to be underneath his comforter where, if he tries hard enough, he might be able to pretend that no piss had run down his leg, and no old lady had been staring out her window, and no father had gone into Herb's Hideaway as one person and then emerged as another. He might pretend too that Pete's handshake had been real and he could walk to school tomorrow and every day after without ever having to look over his shoulder again.

An approaching vehicle turns on its high beams.

"You're too far over," Wayne says.

His father snaps out of it and torques the wheel and gets the car back into its own lane as the other vehicle goes by.

Wayne looks back and sees brake lights and then

the car that's just passed is turning around and the person driving is reaching out and placing something on the roof, and that something's a siren and it's flashing and the car's coming in their direction.

"Jesus Christ," his father says, pulling over to the curb.

The ghost car stops behind them and the police officer switches on the cab light and sits there for a moment, staring ahead, then reaches over and grabs his hat and puts it on and gets out of the car and he must be seven feet across and it's hard to tell if he's got a neck.

A hard grip on his leg then, just above the knee, and his father's saying, "Not a word."

Wayne nods.

Then knuckles rap against the window.

# FIVE

"Bastard!" Wayne's mother shouts.

His father sits down at the kitchen table and tries to wipe away the ink on his fingertips.

"And Wayne in the car, too," his mother says.

His dad can't seem to lift his head.

"Kill yourself, go ahead, but your *own son*! Not to mention someone else's son. You should be ashamed of yourself."

Wayne tries to make it to the hall, but his mother's voice stops him.

"All over the road was he, Wayne?"

Wayne turns but doesn't say anything.

The front door opens and it must be Wanda back from somewhere.

His mom glares back at his dad. "Suspended licence and there'll probably be a fine and a trial and I hope they lock you up and throw away the key!"

"You'd like that, wouldn't ya?" his father says.

"What?"

"I said, you'd like that, wouldn't ya?"

Wayne stares at his mother and thinks that if she were within arm's length of a fork or cutting board or frying pan, she'd send it flying.

"Who saw, Wayne?" she says.

"No one," says his father.

"'No one'—just listen to him. Everyone sees everything *here*."

"No one saw, eh Wayne?" says his father.

Wayne shakes his head. Then Wanda comes in and her music's blasting and she makes her way to the fridge but then stops. Switches off her iPod and takes out her earphones. "What's going on?"

"Your father's a drunk, that's what's going on," Wayne's mother tells her.

Wanda nods and opens the fridge door and peers inside and then looks back at their mother like she's seen the ghost of Christmas Past. "Is there Diet Coke?"

His mother shakes her head. "Ask your father to drive over and get some— No, wait ... he doesn't have a *licence* anymore!"

His father looks up and goes to say something but thinks better of it.

"What am I supposed to drink?" Wanda says.

"Water, like everyone else," their mom says.

Wanda shuts the fridge door. "I ... AM ... NOT ... DRINKING ... WATER!" Her eyes brim with tears.

"That's all any of us will be drinking after your no-good-for-a-father is finished paying his fine."

His dad stands and knocks over his chair.

"I hate this house," Wanda says, stomping to her room with such force that the salt and pepper shakers above the stove tremble, then she slams her door and one of them—the salt—falls over like a felled tree.

His father picks the chair up and sits back down, and his mother grabs the phone and presses some numbers, then kills the call and presses more numbers and says she's arranging a place to stay while the divorce is being settled.

Wayne leaves the kitchen and walks down the hall to his sister's room and knocks on the door, but Wanda won't answer, so he keeps knocking until finally she opens the door a crack and says, *"What?"*

Her eyes, cheeks, and neck are red.

"Can I come in?"

Something breaks in the kitchen and then his father says, "I won't be buying another one of those!"

Wanda steps out of the way so Wayne can go in, then she closes the door and stands with her back against it and says, "I'm not crying because of Diet Coke."

Wayne sits on her bed.

"And I don't give a shit that Dad was drinking and driving, if that's what they're fighting about … Is it?"

Wayne nods. "They took his licence and finger-printed him and Mom had to come and pick us up."

She pauses. "You were with him?"

Wayne nods.

"And you're not pissed off?"

"Should I be?"

"What if he got into an accident and you ended up in a wheelchair or, even worse, a vegetable, or dead?"

Wayne keeps quiet.

A shout from the kitchen … their mother: "I'll never set foot in this house again!" Then their father: "Promises, promises!"

After a while Wayne says, "Why then?"

"What?"

"Are you crying?"

Another shout from the kitchen … their mother: "I curse the day I ever set eyes on you!" Then their father: "Not a moment's peace since I put that goddamn ring on your finger!" Then their mom laughing and saying: "It was the *bottle* you married!" Something else smashes and their father says: "I won't be buying another one of those *either!*"

Wanda suddenly turns and opens the door and

screams, *"SHUT UP!"* then closes the door again and goes over and sits down beside Wayne. "I'm leaving," she says.

He looks at her. "You are?"

She nods.

"When?"

Wanda wipes her nose. "That's the thing. It was supposed to be the end of the month, but now— seeing as Stephanie's changed her stupid mind—I don't know." She pauses. "Goddamn her! She says she's in months ago, so we're saving up our money: me taking extra babysitting shifts for Greg and Mona and their two little retards, and Stephanie working evenings in her father's parish, and we're all ready to go, right: take the train to Sept-Îles on Saturday and then make our way to Montreal and then Toronto, but no, Stephanie can't go now because her father found her stash of money and asked if she was into drugs, so the stupid cow goes and tells him everything, and now her dad and mom won't let her out of their sight and she has to pray every evening for God's forgiveness. Sure, they kicked me out of the house and everything ... her father there in his clerical collar and holding his Bible and calling me the devil— *Me!* Can you believe it? And here I am, after sneaking over a six-pack of wine coolers, which the stupid cow Stephanie ended up drinking most of."

Heavy footsteps in the hall and a slamming door and something being knocked over.

"I suppose I could go myself, but that wouldn't be too smart, would it ... hot piece of gear like me, and you know what those Frenchmen are like." Wanda breathes out like someone fed up with the world. Unzips her jacket. "So that's why I was crying: freedom at my fucking fingertips, but now I gotta stay here longer and listen to the likes of them."

No one speaks for a while, then Wayne says, "So you've decided to quit school?"

"Why not? It's not like I'm going to be prime minister, right. I failed home economics. Who flunks home economics for God's sake! By the way, you mention a word to the folks and I'll skin ya. Anyway, like I was saying, education's more your thing. Me? I was hoping to get a salon going up in Toronto. Well, me and the stupid cow Stephanie were hoping to. Our idea was to make it alternative: shaved heads and piercings and tattoos and whatnot. And we wouldn't hire any high school graduates, only people like ourselves. And we'd call it Dropout Zone Hairstyling. You like it? Well, do you? I came up with the name on my own. No help from stupid cow Stephanie."

The faint sound of running water.

"He'll fill the kettle and then fall asleep in the rocking chair," Wanda says.

Ages pass.

Wanda says, "Listen."

"What?"

"Just listen. Hear it?"

"I don't hear anything."

"Exactly."

They just sit there.

"I'll miss you when you go," Wayne says finally.

Wanda pauses, then goes to say something but stops herself. Tries again. "You'll leave too one of these days and all those jerks that pick on you will still be here hanging around the corner store trying to pick up girls half their age. I'd beat the Jesus out of the lot of them, but what good would that do you?" Wanda goes silent for a second. "You think there might be one in the crisper that I didn't notice? Or behind the condiments or something?"

"What?"

"Diet Coke? I'm jonesing. Never mind. What was I saying— Oh yeah, those dickwads that pick on you: look, I'm sorry I'm not around much anymore but that doesn't mean I don't have your back, little brother. And hey, when I've got my studio up and running you can get out of this shithole and come visit and have your hair done for free. Hmm … let's see, a nice Mohawk would look awesome on you."

"No way."

"Or a perm."

"You're not touching my hair."

"Don't trust me or what?"

"Not with my hair, no."

Wanda stands up and takes off her jacket and hangs it up in her closet. "All right, get out."

Wayne heads for the door.

Wanda blocks his way.

"What?" he says.

"Remember: you mention anything I told you to Mom and Dad and I'll cut out your tongue. Got it?"

Wayne nods.

"Okay then." Wanda opens the door and Wayne steps into the hall and heads for his own bedroom and hears singing. His father, that Irish tune he always sings when he's had more than he should. Wayne stops and listens and it occurs to him that his father has a nice voice. Strange he hadn't noticed before. Then the song's finished and his father starts from the beginning but then abruptly stops. Wayne goes into the living room and sees his dad slumped over in the rocking chair, so he heads to the kitchen and takes the kettle off the stove and stands there for ages, then goes back to his room and sits at his desk and takes out his pen and notebook and writes:

Dear Wanda,

Have you ever seen that show Intervention? Well maybe we could do one for Dad before you go. Whaddya think? You could read your letter first and then Mom and then me. Maybe we could get you off the Diet Coke too while we're at it. Do they have a place for that in the mountains somewhere? I've never heard of one but there must be something because there's a place for everything else.

I was thinking that when you go the shouting will be even louder with one less person in the house to suck up the sound.

I don't say a lot sometimes or maybe I say too much but you're an okay sister and I didn't know you had my back, so thanks a lot, I appreciate it.

Do people always leave? You will eventually and maybe Mom too after tonight and Pete The Meat's father left Pete (although I don't know why) and some leave even when they're still here (like Dad and Marjorie's mom), so it's like we're always waiting for the person sitting beside us at supper to be gone at breakfast. This all sounds silly I bet, but I've been thinking about so much lately and sometimes I can't keep everything in my head so I suppose that's why I have to write it all down.

Will you ever come back, Wanda? I suppose not, eh? Why would you? Oh, and by the way, that thing you said earlier about not being cut out for school? Well maybe that's true but it doesn't mean you're not smart. You can talk to everyone and stand up for yourself and people seem to like you and I'd give anything for that.

I'll come and see you Wanda as soon as I'm able and I'll miss you 'cause you've always been two doors down and it's given me comfort to know you're there.

Your brother who gets comfort from having you there,
Wayne Pumphrey

# MARCH

Anywhere But Here

# ONE

Mr. Rollie throws his loafer onstage and knocks over a lamp. Marjorie goes over and picks it up (the lamp, not the loafer) then goes back to where her acting partner, Les Faulkner, is standing.

Mr. Rollie limps towards them. The heel of his multicoloured sock is worn through. He stops near the lip of the stage and holds out his hand. Kendrick, the stagehand, hair down to the middle of his back and repeating grade ten for the third time, appears from stage right and retrieves the director's shoe, placing it in Mr. Rollie's palm.

"Thank you, Mr. Mercer."

Kendrick nods and returns to the wings.

Loafer still in hand, Mr. Rollie says, "Why'd you stop, Mr. Faulkner?"

Les folds his arms and juts his chin towards Marjorie. "Ask her."

Mr. Rollie looks at Marjorie.

"Yesterday I grabbed his arm," she says, "but today I walked over to the chair."

Les licks a few fingers and smooths the part in his hair. "She's sabotaging my performance."

A sound like someone choking from the back of the gymnasium.

Les steps forward, a hand over his eyes to block out the glare from the stage lights. "Problem, Pumphrey?"

Wayne closes his notebook and tucks his Razor Point extra-fine pen behind his ear and says nothing.

"Keep quiet then."

"*Tone*, Mr. Faulkner," Mr. Rollie says.

Les looks like he wants to say more, but instead he turns and walks upstage and applies more spit to his fingers and runs them across his scalp.

Mr. Rollie bends down and puts his loafer back on. "You can't just stop in the middle of a scene, Mr. Faulkner. What happens when we have an audience? Are you just not going to say your lines?"

Les faces forward and makes a show of picking something off his pleated slacks. "If *she* can change things, why can't *I*?"

"But she made the scene better!" goes a voice from the back.

Les looks up. "See, that's why you're not in this

production, Pumphrey: you know nothing about acting!"

"He's your assistant director, Mr. Faulkner," Mr. Rollie warns.

"But I've been in drama since I was six and what's he done other than upset the manger and hit Mary with the frankincense in the stupid pageant last year?"

"Costume was too big," Wayne says.

"That's just an excuse for your lack of talent, Pumphrey!"

"Enough, Mr. Faulkner," says Mr. Rollie, pointing his pinky with the gold ring. "We don't belittle in my rehearsal room, understand?"

The now second best actor (after Marjorie) in the school presses his lips together so tightly they disappear.

Then Marjorie says, "I'll do it like before."

Les's lips reappear and a partial smile lifts their corners.

Mr. Rollie takes off his glasses and massages his eyes and puts them back on and says to Marjorie, "I don't want you to do it like before, Miss Pope. I prefer what you did just now. What did you think, Mr. Pumphrey?"

"Awfully good," Wayne says.

Les's smile vanishes and his eyes become slits.

"Don't be afraid to try new things, Mr. Faulkner. We've almost a month left. There's time."

"I liked yesterday better," Les says.

Mr. Rollie smiles. "Note well taken, Mr. Faulkner, but let's not try to set anything in stone just yet."

Suddenly Julie sweeps in from the wings like a Broadway veteran. "Sorry for interrupting, but are we about done for today?"

"Another skirt at the shopping centre, Miss Snow?"

"No," Julie says, bringing a few fingers to her throat. "It's just that I'm beginning to feel vocal strain and I'd rather not push it."

Paul Stool, lying on a mat near stage left, laughs.

Les says, "But we haven't even gotten to your scenes yet."

"Well, if you could get *yours* right," says Julie.

Les recoils like he's just been slapped. *"Excuse me?"*

"That's enough, you two," Mr. Rollie says. Then to Julie, "Sometimes I question your commitment, Miss Snow."

Julie takes centre stage and puts on a little production of her own. "I'm *totally* committed," she says, and with interlaced hands over her heart, goes, "Nothing's better than being onstage." For the finale, she says, "I even plan on taking courses when I go to university." She nearly curtsies.

No one says anything. Les shoots her a look as if to say, *You'll never make it in showbiz,* and Julie shoots Les a look back as if to say, *You're not all that, buddy.* Then Mr. Rollie tells everyone to go home and to get lots of sleep because tomorrow will be a stumble-through of the first half of the play.

Julie sprints off as if there were a mirror in the distance she could admire herself in, while Les, his nose inclined towards the hanging lights, slips away like a jilted lover. Everyone else filters out like factory workers.

Mr. Rollie throws his script into his briefcase and puts on galoshes and says he can't stay because Adrian's cooking lamb with those adorable baby potatoes and something delicious for dessert that Mr. Rollie suspects is crème brûlée, and he's yet to pick up wine … something Australian, although Chilean will suffice, then he scurries onto the stage like a teenager, saying "See you both tomorrow" before exiting into the wings.

Just the two of them now: Marjorie sitting cross-legged in the centre of the stage, Wayne near the back, hands in pockets.

Neither speaks for a long time.

Finally, Marjorie says, "Adrian's not a she."

Wayne doesn't say anything.

"You knew that, I suppose?"

He nods.

"Someone slashed Mr. Rollie's tires once."

"Really?"

"You didn't know?"

Wayne shakes his head.

"You really do miss a lot, dontcha, Wayne Pumphrey?"

"I don't know. I guess."

"Maybe we're not as alone as we thought," Marjorie says.

Silence.

"Hey, Wayne Pumphrey, how much spit's in Les's hair, you think?"

"Don't know … a Dominion bag full?"

"No, more—a pillowcase."

Wayne walks towards her and licks his fingers and smooths his hair. *"She's sabotaging my performance."*

*"I've been in drama since I was six!"* Marjorie says.

Then, pretending to shield his eyes from the glaring stage lights, Wayne says, *"That's why you're not in this production, Pumphrey: you know nothing about acting!"*

Marjorie lies on her back and laughs and Wayne laughs with her. Afterwards she sits up and plays with the electrical tape on the toe of her sneaker.

Wayne scans the gymnasium like he's lost something.

Finally, Marjorie says, "You didn't nag me about my sneakers this morning."

Wayne looks at her.

"I nearly fell in the parking lot and you didn't say a word."

He says nothing.

"Then I go to mention it, but you look like you're someplace else and I wondered what you were thinking about because normally you notice everything I do."

Wayne looks away again just as the door opens, and it's Mr. Ricketts, the janitor, and he wants to know who's there because he's got mopping to do.

"It's Wayne and Marjorie," says Wayne.

Mr. Ricketts steps forward and peers over the rim of his bifocals. "It's nearly suppertime."

"We were rehearsing," Marjorie says.

"We just finished," says Wayne.

Mr. Ricketts reaches into his back pocket and pulls out a hanky and dabs at his eyes because he has this condition that causes them to leak. "Well, I'd like to mop in private if you don't mind. That's all I need: to miss a spot and have you tattling to the school board and they're just looking for a reason anyway, so then where will I be?"

Wayne looks at Marjorie, then back at the janitor. "We were just leaving."

"Who's there the minute a light bulb is blown, eh? Or when a john overflows because some wise guy thinks it's funny to try stuffing as much toilet paper in there as possible? Me: that's who."

Marjorie stands up and walks stage left and down the stairs and joins Wayne.

"Thirty-odd years I've given 'em, and now these *youngsters* on the school board—because that's what they are, *youngsters*, not much older than yourselves—are telling me it's time to have a rest. So I say: 'I'll rest soon enough! Don't need any help from the likes of you!'" He dabs at his eyes again and puts the hanky away and says, "Going to be good this year? The play?"

"Best yet," Wayne says. "Now that we have her."

"Who's her?"

Wayne points. "Marjorie."

The janitor nods.

"Better than the Hollywood crowd, she is."

"Is she?"

"We'll make the local drama festival for sure, and if we win we'll get to go to St. John's for the provincials."

"Couldn't be worse than last year's," Mr. Ricketts says. "Daphne was slumped over in her chair and I thought she was dead, but she was only sleeping. 'On account of the play,' she said. That and the young one forever running spit through his hair."

"Les," Wayne says.

"Huh?"

"Les Faulkner: the one at his hair."

"Oh. He wouldn't be half bad either if he could keep his hands at his sides or in his pockets or something, not that I'm an expert or anything." He pauses and turns and says over his shoulder, "I'm going to get the mop now, so be gone when I get back, 'cause heaven forbid I miss a spot." He pulls open the door. "I should have them youngsters spend a day with Daphne and see how *they* like it." He leaves, but his voice can be heard trailing off in the hallway. "Drive anyone to an early grave that woman would."

Marjorie and Wayne listen to the old janitor's footsteps recede down the corridor. After a while Marjorie takes a step closer to Wayne and says, "You like this planet, Wayne Pumphrey?"

He tries to answer but is suddenly conscious of their proximity, that were he to jut his head forward and stick out his tongue he might be able to taste the flavour of her flannel shirt or catch a whiff of her body wash or soap or whatever it is she uses.

"Wayne Pumphrey?"

"Hmm?"

"I'm waiting."

"I know, and my answer's yes." Then, "You?"

She crosses her ankles and puts her hands in her back pockets and flicks her bangs out of her eyes and says, "Can take it or leave it."

"Yeah, me too: take it or leave it."

"It's too late to change your answer."

"Well, it's a bit of an odd question, don't you think? I mean, what choice do we have?"

She says nothing.

Wayne looks past her shoulder at the floor-to-ceiling mural designed by last year's graduating class, STANDING ON THE EDGE OF TOMORROW in letters as tall as himself. Beneath the writing is a group of graduates, diplomas in hand and wind in their hair, and there's a huge sun and a clear sky filled with birds, and the graduates are standing on the edge of a cliff and looking down upon a bustling city and it occurs to Wayne that they're not really looking forward to the future so much as dreading it. In fact their smiles look more like winces, their wide, hopeful eyes belying the fear underneath, their erect backs and young knees readying themselves for the leap over and downwards onto the gridlocked parkway. Mashed and crumpled and twisted because what now?

Marjorie's talking to him.

"What?" he says.

"You're different, I said."

"Different how?"

"More serious."

He says nothing.

They collect their things and start for the door.

"Wanna come to Woolworths?" Wayne says.

"What for?"

"Every Tuesday Mom gives me free fries with gravy and Pepsi in a tall glass, and I could share with you." He holds the door for her. She walks past him.

In the hallway, she says, "They have swivel stools, don't they?"

"Can spin around all you like."

Marjorie nods. "Okay then."

# TWO

Wayne's mother puts a basket of fries down between them (the gravy on the side as per Marjorie's request) and two Pepsis full of ice and lime wedges and with bendable, candy cane–coloured straws. She steps back and watches, hands on her hips, hairnet, Woolworths uniform, apron, and name tag.

"A lot of fries here, Mrs. Pumphrey," Marjorie says.

She smiles. Juts her chin in Wayne's direction. "Isn't every day he brings someone to share them with."

Wayne adjusts his straw and takes a sip.

A fat man in a toque and parka comes and sits on a stool at the far end of the counter. Rubs and then blows into cupped hands. "Cold front moving in," he says to no one in particular.

"When isn't there one moving in?" Wayne's mom says.

He laughs and his shoulders bounce and everything on the counter shakes.

"I suppose you'd like coffee?"

"I'd like a *pot*."

Wayne's mother nods. "Be right there." She turns back to Marjorie. "Wayne says you're the best actress."

Marjorie shrugs and dunks a fry in the gravy and takes a bite.

"She's better than the Hollywood crowd," Wayne says.

"Yes, that's exactly what he's been saying: that you're better than all them in Hollywood."

Marjorie's redder than the ketchup. "Well, Wayne's a very good assistant director."

"Is he?"

"Mm-hm. Always jotting away in his notebook."

Wayne's mom looks at him. "He's like that at home. Hunched over his desk writing God knows what."

The fat man coughs and takes off his toque. Unzips his jacket and glances over.

Wayne's mother holds up a finger and says, "One sec," then steps forward and leans across the counter so that her face is close to Marjorie's. When she speaks her voice is a whisper. "How's your mom?"

Before Marjorie can answer, Wayne goes, "She'll know to make the beef chunks smaller from now on."

"What?"

"Nothing, Mrs. Pumphrey. She's fine."

Wayne's mom wipes her hands on her apron. "That's good." She heads over to the coffee pot. "Better not see one fry left over."

"You won't," Wayne says.

She takes the pot over to the man and he thanks her and says again how a cold front's moving in.

Wayne dunks two fries into the ketchup, then into the gravy, finishing them off in one bite. Wipes his mouth with the back of his hand.

The fat man wants a cheeseburger with extra cheese and extra bacon. Onion rings instead of fries. Extra onion rings. He'll pay the difference.

Wayne's mom goes through the swinging doors.

Marjorie says, "It wasn't the beef chunks."

Wayne lets go of his Pepsi and looks at her and waits for ages.

Finally, she says, "Her nerves. Thought she was dying." Marjorie grabs the counter and starts swivelling to the right, then left, and back again.

The fat man adds spoonful after spoonful of sugar to his coffee and enough cream to fill a pastry. His bulk hangs out over the edges of his stool as he stirs and sips, then adds another sugar packet and stirs and sips again.

Wayne says, "How can nerves kill you?"

Marjorie does two complete spins, raising her hands in the air like she's on a merry-go-round, then stops herself and says, "You'd be surprised. I think it's like being depressed."

Wayne stares at his Pepsi for a long time. At last, he says, "Are your nerves bad, too?"

"Don't know. Maybe."

Quiet again except for the fat man's breathing.

A voice over the intercom: "Price check in aisle four."

Wayne fiddles with his straw, then dunks a fry. Keeps dunking it.

Marjorie says, "Trying to drown it?"

He lets go and watches the fry disappear beneath the gravy.

Then his mom appears with two plates. One holds the burger, the other the onion rings. She puts them down in front of the man. "Looks great," he says. "Enjoy," she says back, before disappearing again into the kitchen.

The fat man stuffs onion rings into his mouth and then lifts up his burger bun and grabs the bacon and chews that too, but now he's put too much in his gob and he's choking, so he spits into his napkin and balls it up and rests it beside his plate and then gulps coffee.

Wayne says, "Keep finding these notes … in my

schoolbag, on my desk, my locker. Sometimes I'm in the washroom and there's a note on my back that I didn't know was there. Always the same message: *PAYBACKS COMING PUMPHREY!* There's never an apostrophe and it's always in capitals. He follows me home, too, and he gives me these looks, but they're different, so I can't tell what he's thinking—"

"Price check in aisle four," goes the voice again. "My God, Blanche, will you come to *bloody* aisle four *already!*"

Marjorie says, "Go on."

"I don't know. It's like he's waiting for just the right moment or something." Wayne goes to reach for his glass but changes his mind. "Whatever it is, it's going to be a lot worse than what came before."

They're quiet for a long time.

The fat man licks his fingers.

The intercom voice again: "Never mind, Blanche. Went and did it myself, didn't I?"

Wayne says, "Why does he hate me?"

Marjorie swivels in his direction and stares for ages and then says, "Same reason he hates me: because we don't fit."

Wayne looks past her shoulder at the fat man now picking his teeth with the prongs of his fork and whose plate looks like it's just been put through the dishwasher, then focuses back on Marjorie in time for her to say,

"Because you're odd and small and your eyes are too far apart and you like to write and I'm skinny and I keep the meat department at Dominion in business."

Getting a few crumpled bills from his wallet and setting them beside his plate and getting into his jacket and standing up exhausts the fat man. He leans against the counter for support.

Wayne's mother comes out and collects the money and starts clearing his section and tells him to come again and the man wonders if he's mentioned the weather that's moving in and Wayne's mom says yes, he has, so the man wishes her good evening and waddles away.

Then his mother is standing in front of them, her arms full of the man's plates and cup and utensils and used napkins. "Odd for you to leave so many fries, Wayne," she says before going back into the kitchen.

After a while Marjorie says, "Mom's actually going to be out tonight if you can believe it, so you can come over."

"Really?"

She nods. Then, after a long time, she adds, "I've got something I think you should hear."

# THREE

They're standing in Marjorie's driveway. She's wearing Wayne's toque, hands jammed in her pockets and red cheeks beneath the glow of the streetlight. Purple lips. Icicles for eyelids.

Wayne's hood is up. His fingers—to keep frost-bite at bay—are fists inside his mittens. Breathing's like swallowing shards of glass.

So quiet—not a car or skidoo or barking dog; no bus full of tired miners, their heads slumped against windows in sleep; no street hockey or children in snowsuits and neck warmers, sucking the tips of frozen mittens and building snow forts; no people shovelling their driveways or the walkways to their front doors—nothing ... just the silence that's like being forgotten. Left behind.

Marjorie says, "I can't feel my nose."

"Me neither. Or my ears."

"How long to die from hypothermia?"

"Don't know." He looks up and thinks that the northern lights are cold, too. Why else would they be dancing like that? The stars, it seems, are huddling the moon for warmth.

She says, "Come inside."

"You sure?"

"Yes." She turns and walks to her front door, then says over her shoulder, "Jesus, Wayne Pumphrey, you testing to see how long it *does* take?"

"What?"

"To die of hypothermia?"

He runs over and they go in and it's so dark there's not even an outline of things. A smell like meat left out too long. She tells him to come on and not to bother with his boots.

Taking his hand, she guides him into the dark, through another door and down a staircase and the air's musty like things unwashed and she makes sure he holds on to the rail. The stairs creak and he can feel the cold coming off her and, at the bottom, she tightens her grip and turns right and says, "This way." Along another hallway and a sharp left, then she stops and he nearly bangs into her. She lets go of his hand and he hears her unzipping a jacket pocket and then a key inside a lock and a twisting of a door handle and it being pushed open and then her voice: "Mom says I'd be better off in the sunshine. Like *she's* got room to talk. No one glares at me in here, or whispers behind my back, or calls me slut. And who cares if I am anyway. Probably having more fun than the rest of them."

She guides him in and sits him on a wooden chair and tells him to stay put while she gets the light. He hears straining bedsprings and then a chain being pulled and suddenly the room's awash in red and it's like being in a dream. There are posters of bands he's never heard of on her walls and who's Thom Yorke? A dresser's in the corner with its drawers hauled open and a disc player's on top and CDs are scattered everywhere. The bedspread's red too, as is the carpet and the colour of her walls. Her desk's strewn with magazines and a biography of Dakota Fanning and *The Outsiders* and there's a picture in a frame too and it's of a smiling, unshaven man in a sweater and a tweed cap leaning against a fence with crossed arms.

Marjorie shrugs off her jacket and kicks articles of clothing underneath her bed, saying, "I'm far from a clean freak." She goes over to the CD player and puts in a CD and presses play, and then sits on the edge of her bed with her hands on her knees and her face towards the wall with closed eyes.

Wayne listens and the song's sort of haunting-sounding and lonely and he looks over at Marjorie and she's bobbing her head and stomping her foot and mouthing the words and it's like nothing he's ever heard before and he thinks he likes it, but he isn't sure. Then she's turning up the volume and telling him that her favourite part is coming up, and then she's on her feet and pointing towards the music, saying, "Here it comes! Listen! Just listen!" Eyes closed again and now she's bouncing at the knees and swaying her head, and if her hair were longer, Wayne thinks, it would be flying.

He doesn't catch all the words, but the ones he does hear talk about being a weirdo and not belonging anywhere and then he lifts his head and Marjorie's staring right at him and she's nodding and her eyes are glistening and she says, "Well?"

He pauses. "Well what?"

"Whaddya think?"

He shrugs. "It's good."

She lowers the volume. "*Good!* That's all you can say? It's better than good, Wayne Pumphrey, it's *great* is what it is. It's everything—it's you and me and being creeps and wondering what the fuck we're doing here and how there must be somewhere else. It's like Thom Yorke is singing just for me."

Marjorie points to one of the wall posters. "Thom Yorke: the lead singer."

"Oh."

Marjorie sits back down and lets the rest of the song play out before turning down the volume a bit more and saying, "Whole album is amazing, but 'Creep' is the best."

Wayne looks again at the picture on Marjorie's desk.

"Dad," she says. "Radiohead was his favourite and this CD is the most important thing he left me."

Wayne slides forward in his chair to get a better look.

"He was young when it was taken. Not that he ever got old."

"He looks like you."

"I look like *him*, you mean?"

"Yeah—that."

"He smiled all the time. But he wasn't happy."

Wayne looks at her.

Marjorie turns her face away then makes herself more comfortable by resting her back against the headboard and taking off her sneakers and crossing her feet at the ankles. "You can take your jacket off, you know."

Wayne does, draping it on the back of his chair, then says, "Where did you say your mom was?"

"Group."

"Group?"

"Yep."

"What's that?"

"People get together and talk about their dead loved ones, but mostly they cry and blow into tissues and I went once, but it only made me feel worse."

"Oh."

"At least it gets her out of the house." Then, "Tuesdays never come fast enough."

Quiet save for Thom Yorke.

Marjorie shimmies over and pats the spot left vacant beside her. "Why don't you come over, Wayne Pumphrey."

Wayne stays where he is.

"Come over, I said."

"I should go."

"Why?"

"I don't know."

"Go then."

But he doesn't. Then he looks up and her eyes are wet, so he tries to think of something to say knowing somehow that not everything needs to be thought out and that sometimes one should just say what one needs to before the time to say it slips away.

It's Marjorie, though, who, after pressing a palm heel into each eye, speaks first. "It wasn't an accident."

Wayne stares at her for a long time. "What?"

Marjorie lies down and turns on her side and hugs her knees and says, "Come and get me on your way to school tomorrow. If you want."

He doesn't say anything. Then he gets up and goes over and lies beside her. She turns around and faces him and her breath heats his nose and eyelids and her eyes are glossy and huge and something's behind them that Wayne doesn't have words for.

She presses against him, her body a warm quilt. She puts an arm around him. "You're shaking. Are you cold?"

"I'm not sure. Maybe."

"Come closer."

"What?"

"Put *your* arm around me too."

For a long time he doesn't, then he does, feeling ribs and the pumping of her heart and he thinks that, other than his mother and sister, he's never been this close to a girl before. He struggles to hold her gaze.

Ages pass. Then she says, "I keep waiting for him to blast the music and drag me into the living room." She laughs. "He was the worst dancer."

They stay facing each other for the longest time. Then Wayne says, "I'm sorry."

"For what?"

"I don't know."

Radiohead shortening the distances, filling the silences, somehow patching the cracks.

They sleep.

Wayne opens his eyes to see his mother standing there: long coat and matching scarf and a purse clutched against her chest. She's saying something but he can't make sense of it, so he tells her to say it again.

"I said: just what do you think you're doing, mister?"

It dawns on him that he isn't in his own bed and that the woman hovering over him is not his mother after all, but Marjorie's. "Mrs. Pope?"

"That's right, mister, and you still haven't answered my question."

He sits up and gives Marjorie a shake and says, "We weren't at anything, Mrs. Pope."

"Doesn't look like nothing."

"What time is it?"

"Nearly nine."

"We must have fallen asleep."

"Can't sleep at your own place?"

"Mom'll be wondering where I am."

"No *beds*?"

Wayne goes to stand up, but Mrs. Pope holds out the hand with the purse and says, "Not so fast, mister," so Wayne stays where he is.

Marjorie's voice then: "Mom?"

Mrs. Pope looks right at her. "Now I know what you get up to when I'm away—"

"What are you doing in my room?"

"I came in to warm up, Mrs. Pope—"

"You aren't supposed to be in my room—"

"You live down the street," Marjorie's mom says. "And listen to Thom Yorke—"

"Not gonna freeze to death walking down the street!" Then, "Does your mother know what you're up to?"

Marjorie crawls to the foot of the bed and gets to her feet.

"No," Wayne says, "but she wouldn't mind. She encourages me to make friends."

"Lie down with all your friends, mister?"

"Mom!" Marjorie picks up her jacket and sneakers then runs over and takes Wayne's wrist, and as he grabs his jacket she drags him towards the door, but Mrs. Pope gets there first and blocks their way and says, "At least one of us still misses him!"

The hand holding him falls away and the room goes silent and Mrs. Pope clutches her purse against her like it's the only thing keeping her guts in and she tries to speak, but can't, so she swallows and tries again and says, "I didn't mean it. You know me: speak before I think."

"Move," Marjorie says.

Her mother doesn't. "Someone new came tonight. A woman. Not a word out of her."

"*Move*, I said."

"Stared at the floor and played with her necklace and holes in the knees of her jeans, then the meeting was done and she was still sitting there."

"Behind the curtains is the proper place for you," Marjorie says.

Silence.

Mrs. Pope is all whites of eyes and no pupils and lower jaw on her chest. "What a thing to say ... your own mother."

Marjorie turns to Wayne. "Now you know why I never invite you in." Then back to her mother, "One day I'll leave—"

"Don't say that—"

"And never come back—"

"I'd be lost—"

"Then you'll *really* be alone—"

"Am without your father, but without you I'd be worse."

Marjorie's got his wrist again and she pushes past Mrs. Pope and leads him into the hallway and towards the stairs and her mother says, "Didn't have to take my arm off!" Marjorie's taking the steps two at a time and telling Wayne to hurry up because there's somewhere she needs to go and does he want to go with her?

Mrs. Pope is right behind them and she's telling Marjorie that Wayne doesn't have to rush home because, yes: it is cold, especially with the wind.

In the kitchen now and Marjorie takes something
from the cupboard above the fridge and slides it in
her back pocket and it looks like a flask or a bottle
of something and Mrs. Pope tells her to put it back
but Marjorie won't.

"Where are you going?" Mrs. Pope wants to
know.

"Wherever you're not" is Marjorie's reply.

"You'll perish!"

"Then I'll perish!"

Into the foyer and Mrs. Pope is holding on to
the coat rack because she'd fall down otherwise,
Wayne thinks, and she's saying sorry, but Marjorie's
ignoring her and tying double knots in her sneaker
laces. Then she's at full height again and she's
pushing open the door and letting the wind in and
it's sharp like needles and Mrs. Pope comes forward
and drops her purse and says again that she didn't
mean it, that of course Marjorie misses her father,
but Wayne and Marjorie are on the porch, then on
the stairs and the door's flapping in the wind and
Mrs. Pope is standing there and she looks like the
last person in the world and Wayne imagines the
wind taking her somewhere that's closer to where
her husband might be, or at least somewhere where
*everyone* sits in bathrobes and peeks through curtains
and holds tightly on to purses and speaks before
thinking.

Along the driveway and left on Balsam Street and right on Willow and running faster than the cars on Lakeside even, and past the shopping centre, police station, hospital, hockey arena, and curling club, towards the outskirts of town and if Marjorie's not careful she's going to pull Wayne's shoulder from its socket.

They stop and she points at a path through the woods and Wayne says he needs a minute to catch his breath and asks if she was planning on running forever and she says maybe and would he come with her if she were, but he doesn't say.

Sweat running down his back despite the cold. His breath in front of him is thicker than the cloud from the mine.

Jutting his chin towards the woods, he says, "It's dark."

"I know the way, Wayne Pumphrey. Come on."

The snow's deeper on the trail and slivers of moonlight illuminate emaciated spruce trees and ptarmigan prints and maybe fox or wolf, and skidoo and ATV tracks and discarded beer and liquor bottles and cigarette butts.

Upwards now, and it's hard going and Wayne's thighs are burning and there's snow in one of his boots and his toes will freeze before too long and he wonders if she'll ever stop.

The tingle of an earache from where the

wind's getting in. Penis retracted so far inside it's somewhere near his ribs or underneath his liver or pressed against a kidney.

A clearing. A water tower in the centre and it must go up four storeys or more.

"Come on," she says.

Snow up past his knees, hips, waist. He'll drown.

Marjorie's already got her foot on the first rung of the ladder that's attached to the water tower.

"You're climbing it?" Wayne shouts.

"What does it look like, Wayne Pumphrey?"

"What if you fall?"

"I don't know. What if you slip in front of a bus tomorrow?" says Marjorie, heading to the top.

Wayne manages to make it over and he grips the ladder and he can feel the cold through his mittens and he wonders how Marjorie—seeing as she's not wearing any—can bear it. He hoists himself up onto the first rung, then the second, the third, then he looks up and she's kicking her feet and dangling and Wayne shouts for her to hold on, not to let go, that he's coming. Not even thinking about the receding earth now, all his focus on reaching her before she falls. His turn to do the saving, he thinks, but before he can she finds her footing and laughs and says, "You should have seen your face, Wayne Pumphrey!" and he says, "It's not funny!" but she laughs even louder and Wayne continues to follow her to the top and takes her hand when she offers it.

Windier and colder at the top and she sits down on the edge and her feet are hanging out over it and he sits beside her and she reaches back and pulls out what she'd taken from her kitchen and it *is* a flask: Canadian whisky.

Marjorie's hands are shaking from the cold, but she manages to get the cap off and she takes a sip and spits most of it out and tries again and spits that out, too. Then she wipes her mouth and hands the flask over, but Wayne won't take it, so she says, "Suit yourself," and she takes some more and manages to keep it in and even swallow it and it makes her eyes water. She covers her lips with her palm.

"Are you running away?" Wayne says.

She shakes her head. "Escaping for a bit."

He looks down. "We're a long ways up. Shouldn't we move away from the edge?"

"My God, Wayne Pumphrey, is there anything you're not scared of?"

"Yeah."

"What?"

"I don't know."

She takes another sip. Scrunches up her face like it hurts.

"You shouldn't drink."

"Who says?"

Wayne looks away.

Neither speaks for a long time. Then Wayne says, "Take my jacket."

"No."

"You're freezing, and I'm wearing a sweater." Wayne unzips and drapes his jacket across Marjorie's shoulders and she says "Thanks" and then shimmies closer so that Wayne's underneath it a little, too.

They look out at Canning's lights.

"I can see our street," Wayne says. Then, after a while, "It's strange."

"What?"

"To think life's going on down there."

Marjorie sips and coughs and drops the flask and it falls over the edge and she shouts and curses and then shouts some more and kicks her heels against the water tower and Wayne holds her until she stops.

Just the sound of her breathing then, the feel of it against his neck, and he wonders how it could be that yesterday he felt so young but now feels like a man and it occurs to him that something begins at the same time something ends, so he'll always be in motion, moving towards and away from things.

Finally she speaks. "You think it runs in families?"

"What?"

"The bad stuff?"

He doesn't answer.

They look skyward, at the millions of flecks of light, the shaving of moon.

Wayne points and says, "Orion's Belt."

Forever they stare at it.

Marjorie says, "Can you feel old at fifteen?"

"Maybe."

"I hate this town."

"You won't be here forever."

"You heard her: 'Lost without your father, but without you I'd be worse.' How can I go?"

"She'll get better."

"It's been over a year and she's not better yet."

Wayne says nothing.

"Sometimes I imagine it's her that's dead."

Quiet for a long time.

Marjorie says, "Do you think I'm terrible?"

"No."

"You can say if you do."

"I don't."

"I'd think you were terrible."

"I'm not you."

"Lucky."

No feeling in his bum or ears and the ankles of his pants are frozen and he can feel her shivering, so he says "Let's go" but she ignores him and says, "Each day when the train passes through, I see myself hopping on and it never stops and I never need it to."

Wayne doesn't know what to say.

Then a skidoo emerges from the same path Marjorie and Wayne took. Open throttle and a blur of yellow and red and high beams and swirling snow and the driver's holding on for his life, and then it's gone, just like that. Something lost.

The cloud from the mine drifts beside the moon.

All of him is shaking, so he holds her tighter and feels all of her shaking too, then he suggests again that they go and she says it's funny to be shivering and not feel the cold, but yes, she's ready to leave because sometimes the cold has a way of tricking you and it wouldn't be fun to have all your fingers and toes amputated like Jason Saunders who passed out in the snow a few years ago and almost died and who now lives on Fallow Crescent and is on welfare.

Marjorie goes to give Wayne back his jacket, but he tells her to keep it, but she insists, so he takes it back, although she does accept his mittens and scarf.

They climb down the ladder and retrace their steps through the woods to the outskirts of town, past the curling club, hockey arena, hospital, police station, and shopping centre, past the bungalows with the smoking chimneys on Lakeside Drive, and left on Willow Avenue where snowy lawns sport anorexic balsam firs, and finally right onto their street and to Marjorie's house.

A light goes on in the living room. Fingers part the drapes. An eye.

"Sorry about tonight," Marjorie says.

"It's okay."

"She wasn't always like this. I shouldn't have invited you in."

"I liked being there."

"You don't have to say that."

"It's true."

"Okay ... whatever."

Marjorie turns to go.

"Thanks," Wayne says.

She looks back at him. "For what?"

"For showing me the view. You can see everything from the water tower."

She stays quiet.

"I could always see it in the distance," Wayne says, "but it never dawned on me to walk there, let alone climb it."

Marjorie looks at Wayne for a long time, then she comes forward and gives him back his scarf and mittens and walks to her front door and goes in.

The eye disappears and the curtains flutter and Wayne makes his way down the road towards home.

—

Dear Water Tower,

You're a hard place to get to, but well worth the effort. Thanks for the great view and for being colder at your top so that Marjorie had no choice but to snuggle close to me to keep warm. Thank you for bringing us closer to the stars and the moon and Orion's Belt and thank you for being far away and safe and above things and it's just occurred to me that if I can just hang on to this feeling everything will be okay.

You're a long way up, Water Tower, and I had a dream once that I was falling and just before I hit the ground I woke and I heard someone say once that if you didn't wake up you'd die of a heart attack but I doubt it. How can dreams, other than not coming true, kill you?

I told Marjorie earlier that I could always see you but it never occurred to me to climb you and I guess sometimes you can miss what's right in front of you, so maybe I should open my mind instead of just my eyes.

Do you mind if I come back sometime? To think and see things from another perspective and to look out at Canning's lights to remind myself I'm not alone?

Your climber who needs Canning's lights to remind himself he's not alone,
Wayne Pumphrey

Dear Marjorie's mom,

We weren't at anything. Promise. Marjorie was upset so I went over to give her a hug and then the next thing I knew I was waking up and you were there. Nice to meet you by the way.

Listen, Marjorie told me the truth and I'm so sorry and I was wondering if it's worse to lose someone by accident or by the way your husband died, or are both equal? Does one way make you madder? And how sad do you have to be to do something like that do you think?

It's great that you go to that group on Tuesdays. Hope it's helping. Here's the thing, though: I think Marjorie could use some help too 'cause she's still really upset and you've got that meeting but Marjorie's got nothing. And you're wrong about Marjorie forgetting, 'cause I know she's got him in her head all the time even when she says she doesn't 'cause she gets this look. No, if you ask me, she thinks about him TOO much. Is that possible, to miss someone like that? Oh, I was meaning to tell you, I saw his picture and he looks just like Marjorie or rather Marjorie looks just like him, so do you see his face when you look at hers?

How are your nerves now? How come you always sit behind the curtains? It's kind of creepy when you peer out and all I see is this one eye and a few fingers. You looked nice this evening all done up and wearing that coat, is it tweed? Although your hairstyle might be a bit outdated, but my sister could help you since she's opening up her own salon in Toronto. Do you want me to ask?

I don't know if you know but how could you not since you brought her up, but Marjorie's the best actor in the drama club. Our ticket to St. John's Mr. Rollie says. Better than the Hollywood crowd! It's like she's not acting when she acts, does that make sense? She could ~~prbobaly~~ probably be in movies or in SPIDER-MAN on Broadway. Would you like having a famous daughter?

The friend of your daughter who's better than the Hollywood crowd,
Wayne Pumphrey

Dear Marjorie,

I very rarely write three letters in a single sitting but I just wanted to say that I liked lying down with you and—

A knock on his bedroom door.

"Hold on a second."

"Comin' in."

"Hang on!"

... and I've also been ~~thiking~~ thinking more about that song and you're right about us being creeps.

Your friend the creep,
Wayne Pumphrey

The door opens.

Wayne closes his notebook.

"You naked in here?"

"No."

Wanda walks into the room: iPod, track pants, T-shirt, and recently polished toenails. A Diet Coke with a straw in her hand. "Whatcha writing?"

"A letter."

"Email would save you postage, you know."

"I'm not sending it."

"You're not, eh? No point if no one reads it."

Wayne doesn't say anything.

Wanda plops down on the bed. Sips her Coke. "So me and stupid cow Stephanie are going again."

"When?"

"End of May."

"Oh."

"I won't be like Mom: packing my bags till I'm eighty, then it's too late." Wanda lifts a foot and blows on her nails and says, "You like this colour?"

Wayne shrugs.

"I mixed the red and green, but I'm not sure it works."

"What do I know about that stuff?"

"I'll be doing a lot of this sort of thing when I open my own salon: experimenting with colours and hairstyles and whatnot. I think I'll have rock music playing 24/7. Wouldn't you love to get your hair cut in a place like that?"

"I don't know."

"*Everyone* will want to come: actors, hockey players, rock stars. Especially rock stars and they'll all want to date me seein' as I'm a piece of gear and everything, and I'll let them. Be rich, I will. You'll be jealous."

"Whatever."

Wanda gets up and goes to the window and looks out. With her back to Wayne, she says, "Mom said you brought that girl from up the street to Woolworths."

"Marjorie."

"Yeah—her."

"We had fries. Pepsi in tall glasses."

"She your girlfriend?"

"No."

Wanda sips more Coke. "Fuckin' place, eh? Ice and snow and that cloud of iron ore shit and it's so fucking cold you gotta walk back to the wind and why in God's name would anyone choose to live here?"

"I don't know."

Wanda turns around. "They say her mother's not right in the head."

"Hmm?"

"What's-her-name from up the street."

"Marjorie."

"Yeah—her."

"It's on account of her nerves."

"Really?"

"She's depressed."

"Who isn't?"

"Bad nerves can kill you."

"Everything kills you ... living in this house." Wanda goes back and sits on the bed. "I suppose you've heard the rumours."

Wayne doesn't say whether he has or hasn't.

"A friend of a friend's mother—who's a Jehovah's Witness by the way and never lies—says she caught what's-her-name lying beside the deep freeze with her pants around her ankles."

"Shut up."

"Just saying what I heard."

"Shouldn't believe everything you hear."

Silence.

Wanda crushes her Coke can. "Don't breathe a word about me and Stephanie or I'll cut out your tongue. All we need is for her minister father to get wind of it again. Ship her to Bible prison and brand a cross onto her tit or something." Wanda looks down at her feet. "Nope, don't like this colour." She stands up and heads to the door and grabs the knob, but doesn't open it. "She ever mention her own father? What's-her-name from up the street?"

"Marjorie."

"Yeah—her."

"Sometimes."

"What does she say?"

Wayne pauses. "That it wasn't an accident."

Wanda lets the doorknob go. "I heard that too."

Quiet.

"How then?" Wayne says.

"It was pretty hush-hush in the news, but my friend of a friend's mother who's a Jehovah's Witness and never lies says he jumped."

"Jumped?"

"Slipped is what *they* reported, but jumped is what this lady said. For a while they thought he was going to make it, but he died before they could get him to St. John's."

Neither of them speaks for ages.

"Jumped where?" Wayne finally says.

"The water tower." Then, "What's the matter?"

"Nothing."

Wanda puts her earphones back in. "Be careful."

"Of what?"

"I don't know." She presses play on her iPod and pulls open the door and leaves.

—

Dear Marjorie,

Is it true? Did your dad jump? Why didn't you say anything? YOU don't have any intention of doing that, do you?

There I was enjoying Orion's Belt and Canning's lights and I bet all you were thinking about was the man with the smile that had no happiness in it standing on the edge with his head down and his hair blowing and his shaking hands at his sides. Was he wearing his wedding ring, or did he want to pretend that no one other than himself was going to be hurt?

Did he regret it on the way down, do you think, or was there nothing? Did it hurt? Wanda says he lived for a little while so what must have been going through his mind or was he in a coma? But they say you can still hear in a coma, so did he listen to the voices of the ambulance people and the doctors and nurses and your mom and you? Did he wish he could wake up and take it all back and try again, because how bad do things have to be to go and do the likes of that?

Does it bring you comfort to stand in the last place

that he stood? Or does it make you miss him more?
Does it make you want to jump too?

Your friend who wonders if it makes you want to
jump too,
Wayne Pumphrey

# FOUR

Wayne wakes for the second time that night, half-expecting to see Marjorie's mother leering down at him again, but then he remembers he's in his own bed, so he lies there and stares at the ceiling.

Still half-asleep, Wayne kicks off the bedsheets and makes his way to the hall in the dark. Fingertips along the wall guide him. Around the corner and a light's on above the stove and his father is leaning against the counter reading from that book again. A cup of tea and an uneaten molasses tart, and when had his father ever left a molasses tart just sitting there?

His dad lifts his eyes from the page. "What are you doing up?"

"Thirsty," Wayne says, en route to the fridge. He grabs the milk and sets it on the counter and fills a glass and drinks without stopping and some dribbles down his chin and onto his pyjama top. He puts the glass in the sink and starts back to his room, but his father's voice stops him.

"Hang on."

Wayne turns around.

His father goes to speak, but doesn't. Looks down at the floor. Gives it another go. "Has your mother mentioned if she ever plans on speaking to me again?"

Wayne doesn't say.

"It's been ages since the cops pulled me over and she's never gone this long and the foldout's killing my back, so I'm wondering if maybe this thing's permanent."

Silence.

"She hasn't said anything," Wayne says.

"Oh." His father looks away.

Neither speaks for a long time.

The grandfather clock chimes.

His father says, "The fella I talk to says if I keep reading this here book and going to them twelve-step meetings, I'll never have to take another drop."

Wayne stands there and says nothing.

"Would you like that?"

He nods.

"I know: I'm a broken record, but nearly losing stuff changes you, so it's going to be different this time." His dad pushes his tart away. "You shouldn't have been in the car."

"It's all right."

"No."

"I wasn't hurt."

"The sin's not less because it turned out okay." His father closes the book and massages his face and then braces himself against the counter. "Go back to bed."

Wayne goes to leave.

"Just a minute."

He stops.

"There's one more thing."

Wayne waits.

"Naw, nothing, go on to bed—no, stay here, let me just say this last thing and that'll be the end of it and what it is is: I woke up this morning and I didn't regret anything from the night before and I can't remember a time when there was nothing broken I had to sweep up and I've been lying to myself and to all of you, so I'm sorry now go to bed and I mean it this time."

Wayne doesn't go.

His dad picks his book back up and finds where he left off and starts reading. After a while he says, "Can't concentrate with you standing there."

Wayne goes back to his room and climbs into bed and pulls the sheets up and sleeps.

# APRIL

Melting Ice

# ONE

It's three-thirty and Wayne's rushing down the corridor. He stops just inside the main doors and watches the larger-than-normal smoking crowd gathered in the parking lot ... some sitting on skidoos, and others, the older kids, leaning against or sitting in their parents' cars or trucks, elbows resting on the frames of open windows, their jackets unzipped because it's freakishly warm for the second week of April. Instead of fur-lined moccasins and Sorels, everyone's in rubber boots and hiking shoes and sneakers and this morning, on the radio, there was a warning to stay off the thinning pond ice.

Wayne breathes deep and then pushes open the doors and runs, his knapsack cutting to the left and then right with each stride. A voice in the distance says, "Where's the fire, Wayne?" Someone turns up their car radio. He makes it across the parking lot and past the school grounds to the street. He looks back and there's no one. Because the snow is turning to slush his pant legs are soaked, and somehow water has gotten into one rubber boot, freezing his big toe. He runs past snowbanks lightly sprinkled, it occurs to him, with the same iron ore dust that's constantly in his father's moustache and underneath his father's fingernails.

It's being *left alone* since going to Pete's house that's making him run now, he knows. The same thing that made him run yesterday and the day before that and all of last week, and it can't be put into the words of a letter, but it's there.

The sound of an approaching vehicle brings Wayne back, as does the voice saying, "Where you off to in such a hurry, Pumphrey?"

Then the car cuts Wayne off and stops and Pete The Meat's in the passenger side and Bobby's driving. Harvey and Kenny are in the back.

"If I didn't know any better, I'd say you were trying to avoid me, Pumphrey," says Pete.

He thinks about making a run for it and it must show on his face, because Pete says, "Don't even try it."

The Meat licks his almost-a-moustache and says, "Hey, you like Bobby's car? Well, it's his dad's really, but his old man's pulling a double at the mine, so Bobby's got it."

No one says anything.

Then Pete says, "I asked you a question, Pumphrey."

"Yeah," goes Bobby, "Pete asked you something."

"Yes," Wayne says, trying to catch his breath.

"Yes, what?" goes The Meat.

"I like Bobby's car."

Pete smiles. "Yeah, it's not too shabby, eh? Lots of leg room. You should see the trunk." After a while he says, "You didn't think I'd let you get away with it, did you, Pumphrey? Sorry if you got that impression." He turns to the others. "Like I told you boys: he was sitting in my kitchen, eating my Rice Krispie squares. Fucker."

Bobby shakes his head and revs the engine and says, "Pretty stupid thing you did, Pumphrey, going to Pete The Meat's house."

"Should have been there, boys … his father smiling at me and saying that Wayne here's weaker than the rest of us." Pete laughs. "His own *dad* thinks he's a pussy."

Bobby laughs and repeats: pussy.

"Had his old man shaking my hand by the end, I did." Pete looks into Wayne's eyes and says, "Bet your father wishes you weren't such a faggot, eh, Pumphrey?"

"Yeah," Bobby says, "bet that's what he wishes."

Pete opens the car door and gets out and goes

right up to Wayne and pushes him, and although
Wayne goes flying back, he's able to stay on his feet.
Pete pushes him again and this time Wayne goes
down and when he tries to get up The Meat knocks
him over, so Wayne stays where he is, melting snow
soaking his pants.

Pete looks up and down the street, then says,
"We're going to take a little spin, Pumphrey.
Nowhere far, don't worry. Then we'll drop you off
at your house or at Maple Leaf's or wherever."

Harvey and Bobby exchange glances and Kenny
says, "How is she, by the way?" and Wayne goes to
speak, but Pete says, "Tell her that Dominion is
pissed about all their wieners going missing."

"Yeah," Bobby says, "tell her that."

"The cops are going to investigate, what I hear.
She'll have to open her snatch and show 'em the
goods," says The Meat.

Bobby, seemingly enjoying the thought of that
too much, repeats: "Show 'em the goods."

After what feels like ages, The Meat tosses a look
over his shoulder at Kenny, then back at Wayne, and
says, "A snowball's not gonna cut it this time. And
eating yellow snow is starting to get old, don't you
think?"

Wayne stays quiet. His underwear, because of
the wet snow, is soaked now, too.

Pete smooths his almost-a-moustache for a while

and then turns to the car and nods and suddenly doors open and there are slick footsteps pounding in Wayne's direction and he's at once lifted and carried. Kenny's got his feet, Bobby and Harvey each shoulder. Heavy breathing coming from all around him. His insides shaking. Pete's shouting orders: "Hurry up, dickwads! Before anyone sees."

Wayne stares up at the sky, at that middle place between day and night. Always in the middle, he thinks, the land of upside downs and misplaced steps and pointed fingers.

A key fob and a pressed button and the trunk opening like a mouth.

He's airborne for a moment.

He lands.

The world goes black.

It's like being under water. Like he's here, but not, too. Lost somewhere. Muffled voices and he can't breathe and he wishes there was something to latch on to. It's having no legs, being in this trunk, or arms. No means of getting to the surface.

Bobby makes a sharp turn and Wayne rolls and something sharp digs into his back and it's booster cables. Another turn and this time all of Wayne's insides drop into his feet. Now the car's in the air and so is Wayne and he lands hard and his wind is knocked out of him. Hoots and hollers from the front. Someone is smacking the roof with a palm or fist. Now the radio's blaring.

Wayne thinks of what Marjorie said: *Each day when the train passes through, I see myself hopping on and it never stops and I never need it to.* He imagines grabbing her hand and running through snow and iron ore dust, past soot-stained miners with tipped hard hats and unlaced workboots and convenience stores advertising cheap beer and scratch tickets and Coca-Cola, and along the Trans-Labrador Highway into Quebec and then the Trans-Canada down through Ontario and across the border into New York, to Broadway. Maybe they'd run even farther, all the way to Hollywood where Marjorie's better than most of that crowd anyway. They'd rent a place and talk about everything they'd left behind and never go back. No more Pete The Meat and wiener jokes, closed drapes and Bacardi Dark, packed suitcases and feeling bad about things that can't be changed.

The car stops and the radio dies and doors open and close and Pete's laughing and shouting, "Guess who I got in here! Just guess!" Pounding on the roof and more voices—too many to be just Pete and his posse—coming from all directions.

"Not scared in there, are ya?" The Meat says.

Kenny goes, "Bawling like a baby, I bet."

A girl's voice goes, "Who's in there, Pete?"

"Patience, patience," says The Meat. "Gather round everyone." Then, "Hurry on."

"It's not an animal is it?" someone says.

"I hope not," says another.

Pete goes, "It's worse than an animal."

"Is it dead, whatever you got in there?"

"No, but it may as well be."

"Open the trunk!" shouts someone.

"What are you waiting for!" cries another.

Then someone says, "He's bluffing."

Bobby's voice: "You'll see if he's *bluffing*."

"Give you a hint," Wayne hears The Meat say. "It's short and skinny."

"Bobby's dick!" someone blurts out.

Laughter.

"Shut up!" Bobby says.

The Meat asks the crowd if they'd like another clue and someone tells him to pop the Jesus trunk already, but Pete gives one more hint, saying, "His girlfriend likes to stick wieners in her you know what."

Quiet for a moment, then someone—a girl— says, "You're gross, Pete."

"That's rude," says another.

Pete says, "Rude or no, it's the truth."

Wayne feels a sharp pain in his toes, then realizes it's because he's just kicked the trunk.

The Meat's voice sounds closer, as if his mouth were in the place where the key goes in. "That's a touchy spot for you, isn't it, buddy? Perhaps we oughtta go over and pick her up too, eh?"

Wayne kicks the trunk again.

"She could teach you how she does it—"

Bobby shouts, "That's my father's car!"

Wayne isn't stopping, even using his fists now, too.

"Pop the trunk!" Kenny screams.

"Let him out!" someone else shouts.

A shrill, high-pitched voice goes, "Is there any air in there?"

The sound of a key in the lock and Bobby opens the trunk and Wayne's suddenly kicking the air, punching the wind. He expects hands to reach in and grab him, but none do, so he stops and sits up. Fifty or more pale faces staring at him—big eyes and hanging-open mouths and running noses and Treena Cobb with the belly button ring and Paulette King (five months pregnant) with her boyfriend Perry who doesn't care that he's not the father and some members of the volleyball team and some of the alternative crowd and his used-to-be-friend Corey Parrot standing beside Monica and Monica's right: Corey's not too bad looking now that his braces are off.

"It's Wayne Pumphrey," someone at the back says.

A girl cups her mouth.

A fat boy laughs.

Wayne says nothing.

Someone says, "He's going to cry."

"What did I tell you?" Bobby says.

From somewhere to Wayne's left, a voice says, "What a sin."

But Wayne doesn't cry; instead he climbs out of the trunk and adjusts his knapsack and sees that he's right back where he started: the school parking lot.

Pete The Meat steps forward and faces the crowd and says, "Wayne Pumphrey's a rat."

Wayne breathes so deeply he warms his feet.

"And a pussy," Harvey says.

"That's right," Pete agrees. "And he needs his drunk daddy to fight his battles."

"And he pisses his pants, too," Bobby says, laughing.

"And eats yellow snow," Harvey adds.

A few laugh and then it goes quiet and Wayne thinks he understands loneliness. He lifts his chin and starts to walk away, but Pete's there. When *isn't* he?

"We're not done yet, Pumphrey," The Meat says. "The trunk was only half of it."

"Only half of it," Bobby repeats.

Wayne stays where he is, Marjorie's words in his ears: *Same reason he hates me: because we don't fit.*

*Because you're odd and small and your eyes are too far apart and you like to write.*

Pete walks right up to Wayne and says, "Now you have to admit it to everyone, Pumphrey. Stand right there and say you're a pussy and a rat and you piss your pants and eat yellow snow and need your drunk daddy to fight your battles."

Wayne doesn't say anything.

"Go on, Pumphrey—say it."

"Say it, Pumphrey," Bobby says.

Harvey flicks his cigarette into the air.

"Then I'll let you go," Pete says.

Still Wayne doesn't speak.

"Jesus, Pumphrey, do you want it to get worse?" Kenny says. "Just say it why dontcha."

Pete grabs Wayne by the collar and shakes him. "*Say it,* Pumphrey!"

"Leave him alone!" someone shouts.

Harvey faces the crowd. "Who opened their gob?"

No one answers.

"Was it you, Parrot?" Harvey says to Corey.

Corey looks from Harvey to Wayne then to Pete.

The Meat says, "Harvey asked you a question, Parrot—"

"I'm a pussy," Wayne says.

Silence.

The Meat lets go of Wayne's jacket. "Don't tell *me*, Pumphrey, tell *them*."

Wayne turns and faces everybody and tries looking past them but can't, so he goes to that place in his head where yellow snow tastes like creamsicle and whipped snowballs feel like beads of rain, where drawings taped to his locker are works of art and insults are compliments and the faces looking back at him are all Marjorie's face and Wanda's and Mr. Rollie's and whoever else might have his back.

"Nice and loud now, Pumphrey," Pete says. "So everyone can hear."

Wayne takes a half step forward and says, "I'm a pussy."

"Thatta boy," Pete says. "You hear that, everybody? Pumphrey said he's a pussy. Okay, go on."

Wayne tries to swallow but his mouth's gone dry.

"What else, Pumphrey?" says The Meat.

"And I'm a rat."

"Exactly," says Pete. "Little fucker came to my house—I told you. Keep going, Pumphrey … almost there."

Wayne catches Corey's eye and Corey looks away.

A long silence.

"Pumphrey …"

"And I piss … look, I didn't want my dad to go to your place and I wish I could take it back but I can't and I'm sorry."

Someone shuts off their car engine.

The Meat moves so close to Wayne they could touch noses. "This is your last chance, Pumphrey. Say the rest or else."

"You do bad things, but you're not a bad person," Wayne says.

A hush falls over the crowd.

"What the fuck did you say, Pumphrey?" says The Meat.

"That's what your mom told me. When I was sitting in your kitchen. That and your dad left but you don't miss him."

Someone laughs, then shuts up.

A gust of wind.

Bobby says, "I'd zip it Pumphrey if I were you."

Pete can't seem to move and there's something in his eyes and Wayne figures it's *being stuck*—stuck and torn and perhaps the difference between him and The Meat is not so great after all.

Then Wayne's falling and Pete's falling with him and he imagines an end to things—going into something and then coming out different somehow for better or worse. All of Pete's weight is on top of him and an elbow grazes Wayne's chin and a punch glides across his temple. Then suddenly Pete's hauled

off by Bobby and Harvey and Kenny's shouting that
someone's coming and it looks like the principal,
so Pete and his posse take off and everyone else
scatters too, save for Treena Cobb—who's helping
Wayne to his feet and wondering if he was scared
in the trunk because she would have been and Pete
should be stuffed in his own trunk so he knows how
it feels—and Corey Parrot who's wiping the snow
from Wayne's knapsack and saying how he wanted
to help but what could *he* do against the likes of Pete
The Meat?

Wayne says nothing.

Then the principal, Mr. Inkwell, is standing
there in a suit and tie and his shoes are soaked and
he wants to know what happened and Wayne says
that nothing had, except a bit of fun.

Mr. Inkwell stares for ages, then asks Wayne to
join him in his office.

---

Dear Mr. Inkwell,

I couldn't tell you the truth because then you'd
want to have a word with Pete and his posse and you'd
probably suspend them and it would only make things
worse. It's like I tried to explain to Dad but he wouldn't
listen and that's why Pete put me in the trunk and tried
to get me to say all those things. So I told you that I'd

asked The Meat to show me something I saw in the
UFC and when he did we both fell because it's slippery
in the parking lot with all the ice melting. You sat back
and said my story was shaky and I looked you in the
eye and told you I was sticking to it and you let me
go and said you'd be monitoring the situation and I
nodded and opened the door and found myself getting
sick, so I ran to the bathroom and threw up and I think
it was from all the stress.

I walked home along back roads and skidoo trails
and ignored Mom when she asked why my pants were
wet and I'm so humiliated and it's just occurred to me
that it'd be better if I wasn't here, and no, that's not a
tear that just fell and is making the ink run. Well, okay,
it is, but it's not because I feel sad. I don't feel much of
anything.

Three years! That's a lifetime when Pete The Meat's
walking in my direction or waiting behind the corner
or holding me down so I can't breathe. Three years is
how long before the sun burns out and the earth dies
and everything goes back to the way it was before it all
started.

Three years is forever.


Your member of the student body who thinks three
years is forever,
Wayne Pumphrey

# TWO

It's the next day and Mr. Rollie is standing centre stage, hands on hips and chewing his bottom lip with his eyes on his loafers. Everyone else sits in a circle around him. Everyone but Marjorie. He looks up. Uses his pinky to remove something from the corner of his eye. Goes to speak but stops himself, then tries again. "No easy way to say this ..."

Everyone waits.

Wayne can't breathe.

"... so I'll just come right out with it." But Mr. Rollie doesn't, preferring instead to walk the circumference of the circle while scratching his neck and moaning softly.

Julie gets to her knees and cups her mouth as if waiting for someone to confirm her winning Lotto numbers.

Les smooths his hair.

Jason and Shane give up comparing boob drawings.

Mr. Rollie stops. Raises his hands in surrender before letting them fall lifelessly at his sides. Then he says, "She quit."

Sixteen—save for Wayne—intakes of air.

Mr. Rollie's bottom lip quivers.

Then Kendrick drops the electrical tape he's been holding and it rolls off the stage and onto the gymnasium floor, then along the aisle, finally coming to a stop against a chair leg where it wobbles for a second before falling over on its side. For a moment everyone keeps looking, as if it might somehow regain its former momentum and roll straight out the door and along the corridor and out into the parking lot. Perhaps it might roll forever. All eyes go back to Kendrick.

Kendrick stares at the ceiling.

Julie raises her hand.

Mr. Rollie doesn't even say her name, just points.

"I just want to say that it's awful what she did, especially since the opening is tomorrow night, but on the bright side, I've learned all her lines and am ready to take over should you need me." Julie shoots Les a grin.

If Les's smile were any wider it would be wrapped around his earlobes and dangling like earrings.

Mr. Rollie exhales like someone accustomed to

things not working out, then takes off his glasses and puts them back on, and says, "I suppose we've no choice."

Julie screams (she can't help herself) and Les starts clapping like he's at a rock concert.

Sharon, despondent, pulls out a Snickers.

A sliver of a voice then: Wayne's.

"What was that, Mr. Pumphrey?" Mr. Rollie says.

Wayne repeats what he said, but Mr. Rollie still can't hear over Les's clapping, so he tells Mr. Faulkner to stop and Les does.

Wayne stands up. "I said ... someone should go and get her."

Julie says, "It's too late now." She looks at Mr. Rollie. "I'll need her costume pants hemmed."

Wayne slams his notebook closed; the sound reverberates off the walls.

All eyes on him.

Unaccustomed to having everyone's attention, Wayne drops his notebook. He bends over and picks it up and sees that his hands are shaking. He walks into the centre of the circle and says, "Who wants to go to St. John's?"

Everyone raises their hands.

Then Wayne says, "Well, she's our only hope."

Les spits out a puff of air.

"Excuse me?" Julie says.

Sharon's got peanut on her face.

"I'm as disappointed as you are, Mr. Pumphrey,"
Mr. Rollie says.

"Nothing to be done about it now," Les says.

"No—nothing," says Julie.

"But she's better than the Hollywood crowd and
it's impossible to take your eyes off her when she's
onstage and you all know it."

"It was her choice," Mr. Rollie says.

"No."

"Yes, Wayne Pumphrey," Julie says.

"Don't call me that."

"That's your name isn't it?"

"It's her calling," Wayne says.

Les laughs.

Julie rolls her eyes.

Wayne turns to Mr. Rollie. "Those were *your*
words."

Mr. Rollie doesn't seem to know what to say, so
Wayne goes, "If you could spend time in Marjorie's
place you'd understand why she'd never quit, why
she prefers here to there: because Tuesdays can't
come fast enough and her father will never grow
old, so she lives in the basement and sings along
with Thom Yorke, and we're just alike because I'd
rather be here, too!"

It's silent for a long time.

Then Mr. Rollie says, "Do you think you could
get her back, Mr. Pumphrey?"

Wayne's about to say yes, but Les shouts, "We don't need her!" and then Julie says, "We can do it on our own!" and then someone at the back stands up and it's Kendrick and he says, "St. John's is close to the ocean and I've never been close to the ocean and I'm only a stagehand and know nothing about acting, but Marjorie seemed like our best chance, so I'd love for Wayne to go and get her because it's likely I'll never leave this place."

Shane claps.

Jason puts his middle finger and thumb in his mouth and whistles.

Paul Stool actually sits up.

A few of the younger cast members start chanting Marjorie's name.

Sharon says to Wayne, "Give you a Snickers if you can bring her back."

Mr. Rollie puts his hand on Wayne's shoulder. "Didn't I tell you, Mr. Pumphrey?"

"What?"

"That you're a leader?"

Wayne doesn't say anything.

"Go, Mr. Pumphrey. Get her if you can!"

A sea of cheering erupts as Wayne jumps off the stage and runs towards the double doors.

# THREE

Mrs. Pope opens the door and stares at Wayne and tightens the knot in her bathrobe. "What can I do for you, mister?"

Music somewhere. Radiohead.

"Marjorie home?"

Mrs. Pope grips the doorknob. "What's this about?"

"Can I speak with her? It's urgent."

"Urgent? What's urgent at your age?"

"I hear Thom Yorke coming from the basement, so can I just go down and say hello?"

"Not until you tell me what this is about."

Sweat's trickling down his back. "Our show is tomorrow night and she quit, so how can we do it without her?"

"Show? What show?"

"Our play, and if it's good enough to win the

local drama festival—which it will be so long as Marjorie's in it—we'll get to go to St. John's."

"Whoa there, mister, I didn't hear anything about no play."

"She never told you?"

"Told me? What does she tell *me*? Nothing."

"Marjorie's the lead and she's better than the Hollywood crowd and she's so real it's like she's not even acting."

"St. John's did you say?"

"She makes Mr. Rollie cry and she's like light-ning: you can't take your eyes off her—"

"What am *I* supposed to do while *she's* in St. John's?"

"And she smiles. How often have you seen her smile lately?"

"You'd better go now."

"And it's her 'calling.'"

"What?"

"To be onstage."

"Off you go."

"And it gives her something else to think about besides her father."

Silence then, a blast and the dust's settling.

Then the door closes in Wayne's face and the light goes off in the foyer and he imagines Julie putting too much emphasis on words that should be Marjorie's; Les delivering half of his lines to the pretty girls in the front row; Sharon sucking on a Snickers; Paul Stool's erection banging into every-thing; Mr. Rollie with his head in his hands, saying, "So much for St. John's, Mr. Pumphrey."

He turns and walks down the porch steps and along the driveway and he looks and sees the finger parting the drapes and the eye and the bit of chin and mouth and suddenly he's going back and he's taking the stairs three at a time and he's pushing open the door and not bothering with his boots and running through the kitchen and towards the door leading to the downstairs.

"Just what do you think you're doing, mister!" Marjorie's mother says, but Wayne ignores her and runs down the steps and along the hall towards Thom Yorke's voice and stops at Marjorie's door and tries to open it, but it's locked, so he hammers on it, then kicks it, then Mrs. Pope is on the stairs and she's holding the hem of her robe so she doesn't trip and shouting something, although Wayne can't make out the words.

Now Mrs. Pope is in the hallway and Wayne gives the door a final kick and it suddenly opens and a hand grips his own and pulls him inside and Marjorie quickly turns the deadbolt and the music's blasting and her mother's banging on the other side of the door and threatening to call Wayne's parents or, better yet, the police.

She takes him over to the unmade bed and they sit down and Marjorie's father's picture is there and some letters and some five-dollar bills and two twenties and a container of coins and a knapsack that's half packed.

Thom Yorke sings the chorus of "Creep."

Marjorie stands up and goes over and lowers the volume and her mother's about to come through the door she's banging so hard.

"Go away!" Marjorie says.

"Let me in!"

"In a minute!"

*"Now!"*

"I need to talk to Wayne!"

"Tell him he's in trouble!"

"Go away!"

"I'm calling his mother! Maybe the cops, too!"

"Leave us alone!"

More smacks against the door.

Then silence.

Marjorie goes back over to Wayne. She doesn't sit. "You shouldn't be here."

"Where you going?"

"Didn't you learn anything from last time?"

"Why you packing?"

"Shush."

"Sorry." Then, in a whisper, "Why you packing?"

"I don't know, Wayne Pumphrey, why do people usually pack?"

"But where can you go, you're just a kid."

"I'm fifteen and older than people twice my age."

Wayne pauses. "You quit."

"What?"

"We're about to do a dress rehearsal and there's no you, and of course Julie and Les couldn't be happier, but you should have heard the rest of them: chanting your name and clapping and telling me to come and get you and bring you back because we don't have a prayer without you, but now you're going, so what odds."

"Shush!"

"Sorry."

Quiet for ages.

"Come with me," Marjorie says.

"What?"

"Tomorrow night. Train pulls out at eight."

"I can't."

"Afraid, Wayne Pumphrey?"

"No—yes, I don't know. We've got the play and everyone's worked so hard, including yourself, and just how do you think you're going to survive wherever it is you're going?"

Marjorie picks up her father's picture and wraps it in a flannel shirt and stuffs it in her bag. "I'll make beaded necklaces."

"Beaded necklaces?"

"Or I'll act in plays. I'm better than the Hollywood crowd, right?"

"Yes, but you've got what … fifty, sixty dollars? How far's that going to get you?"

"Far enough. Any place is better than here."

"Why?"

"Why what?"

"Are you going?"

"You really have to ask? Because I'm sick of being told I don't miss Dad and I hate her needing me so much and I'm tired of the stupid play and I was there yesterday, Wayne Pumphrey."

A pause.

"What?"

"In the art room and I went to the window and what do you think I saw?"

Wayne can't speak or look at her.

"I wanted to come right through the window and gouge out Pete's eyes but I couldn't because he was making you say those terrible things and I was frozen and *Jesus* Wayne Pumphrey, when are you going to stand up for yourself!" She swipes some CDs off her dresser and goes over and stuffs them into her bag and says, "So that's why I quit the stupid little play: because you'll still be *you* afterwards and I'll still be *me*." Marjorie turns away and walks to her desk and pulls out the chair but doesn't sit on it. She looks back at Wayne. "Just go, all right?"

"Who else are we supposed to *be*?"

"I've got to finish packing."

*"Who?"*

"Never mind!" Marjorie goes back over to the bed. "Get up."

"Why?"

"You're sitting on my jeans."

Wayne stands and Marjorie grabs the jeans and stuffs them into her bag and zips it up.

"We're all depending on you."

"Well, don't!"

"Pfft, you say *I'm* afraid."

"What's that mean?"

"I know it's just a *stupid little play* but how do you know for sure we'll both be the same afterwards? My dad's reading a *stupid little book* and he's not the same. And my neighbour, Miss Flynn, had a *stupid little tummy tuck* and she's not the same either. Well, she also had a nose job and an implant in her chin and her cheeks lifted too, but you know what I mean. Maybe the *stupid little things* change us the most. Why are you laughing?"

"Because you're hilarious, Wayne Pumphrey."

"No, I'm not."

"Yes you are. You're a riot. And you're also the strangest person I ever met."

"Why am I strange?"

"That would take more time than I got, Wayne Pumphrey."

"Fine then! Quit! Go hop on a *stupid little train* and sell your *stupid little necklaces* and have a *stupid little life,* see if I care!"

Wayne goes to the door and tries to pull it open, but it won't budge.

"Deadbolt," Marjorie says.

Wayne slides the deadbolt across and looks once more at his only friend, then walks back down the hall and up the stairs and into the kitchen where Mrs. Pope is sipping tea at the table. She shakes her head and says, "How brazen are you, my son? Barging in like that! Haven't called your mother yet, but I will. And the cops, too!"

Wayne heads to the foyer and throws open the door and runs for home.

———

Dear Marjorie,

I didn't ~~meen~~ mean to say I didn't care about you hopping on a train and selling necklaces and living a stupid little life. I do care. TOO MUCH. But you've let us all down, so why would you do that? You're a great actress but what good if no one SEES you act?

You're so tough, aren't you? Don't need anything or anyone and you can make it on your own with

only fifty or sixty dollars, but you're not so tough and
you're not twice your age, so stop saying you are and
you're right: I've got to stand up for myself, it's just that
sometimes I don't feel like I'm worth very much so it's
hard to fight.

You're not the centre of the ~~univearse~~ universe you
know and sometimes you can hurt people and you've
hurt the whole drama club and especially Mr. Rollie.
Because of you, Kendrick won't stand beside the ocean
and Mr. Rollie won't be able to see his play on the
big stage in St. John's and I won't get to see a sky that
doesn't have an iron ore cloud in it or understand that
there's a world beyond this stupid little town. So right
now ~~I HATE YOU!!!~~

No, I don't. I don't hate you. Not one little bit.
I'm just angry that you're not following your calling
because if everyone did that there would be no Georges
St-Pierres or Oprah Winfreys or Sidney Crosbys or
Jack Laytons so what would be the point in striving for
anything?

I like you so much but sometimes the things you
do don't make sense and you're so dark that you make
me dark too and why can't you change your way of
thinking and be bright instead? When I think of how
close we were to a plane ride and to you standing
underneath the stage lights and having a standing
ovation, I could just cry. I could.

Before my dad quit the bottle my mom would always say her heart was breaking and I couldn't understand how a heart could break, but now I do.

Your friend who understands how a heart could break,
Wayne Pumphrey

# FOUR

It's opening night and Wayne's peeking through the slit in the curtains to find the gymnasium half full already: husbands in the process of removing wives' jackets and draping them across the backs of chairs, while they, the wives, smooth dresses and styled hair and dab the corners of shiny lips. Programs—opened and closed and folded in half and stuffed in pant pockets—sound like fluttering leaves, while children, seemingly too young to sit silently, run amok in the centre aisle.

In front of the stage the band warms up its instruments. Jim Butt twirls his drumsticks while pounding the bass; Melvina Gall mistakenly releases the spit valve of her trumpet onto her nice pants; Brendan Hearte seems to have gotten his hand stuck inside his French horn; and Mrs. Cooper, the music teacher, tries to cover the run in her tights while shouting last-minute instructions.

A hand touches his shoulder. He turns around. Mr. Rollie's there in a three-piece suit and a new earring and smelling like Bounce. "Going to be a good crowd."

Wayne nods.

"Nervous?"

Wayne nods again. "You?"

"Didn't sleep a wink." Then after a while he says, "You did all you could, Mr. Pumphrey."

Suddenly Kendrick appears and he's all in black and his hair's tied in a ponytail and he's wondering if it's time to call places.

Mr. Rollie shakes his head and Kendrick goes to leave, but he stops and says, "Not much chance of getting to St. John's now."

Wayne and the drama teacher exchange glances.

"Never know," Mr. Rollie says. "What do you think, Mr. Pumphrey?"

"No," Wayne says, "you never know."

Kendrick does a poor job of smiling and then exits into the wings.

The band kicks in. Wayne peeks again. Jim Butt's going *tappity tap tap* on the hi-hat while the trumpets scream; Dean Dunn with the blind left eye is doing a fancy lick on the lead guitar as the saxophones slip in all cool and confident. Clarinets in there somewhere, and flutes, but Wayne can't hear either.

Mr. Rollie says, "Perhaps you ought to check on everyone."

"Just thinking that," Wayne says, letting go of the curtain.

Wayne walks into the wings and stops in front of Sharon. She's sitting on a prop stool holding a Snickers. A chocolate moustache that could rival Pete's almost-a-one.

"Your lip," Wayne says.

"Hmm? Oh." She wipes it off using her own spit, then says, "My stomach's rolling."

"Just your nerves."

"And this wig's ridiculous. My own hair so bad they gotta put me in the likes of this?"

"It makes you look older."

"It's loose. What if I go out there and it falls off?"

"Try not to move your head."

"It's pointless without Marjorie anyway."

"Don't say that."

"The drama festival's in a week and you know how good the Catholic school'll be, so we're doomed."

Wayne doesn't say anything.

"Did you know you could buy Snickers in bulk in St. John's? For cheap, too. But *I'll* never know, will I?"

"Just do your best, Sharon."

"Right."

"The band's started and Kendrick will be giving places soon, so good luck."

"We'll need more than that."

Wayne continues towards the backstage area. It's dark and he nearly steps on a prostrate Paul Stool.

"Watch out why dontcha!" Paul says.

"Sorry—"

"Nearly stepped on my head."

"Didn't mean to."

"That would have been nice, wouldn't it: me going out there with a head wound."

"Just wanted to let you know that places will be called soon, so break a leg."

"What?"

"Break a leg."

"Nice thing to say, Pumphrey."

"That's what everyone says."

"Really? The first I heard of it."

Wayne steps over Paul and Paul says that that's bad luck and Wayne says he'd never heard of that being bad luck to which Paul replies, "Well I got a brother who's a minister, so he should know, right?"

Wayne moves on. Up ahead he runs into some of the younger cast members. "Just wanted to let you all know that we're starting soon," he says.

Shouts and giggles erupt and one girl holds hands with another girl and they jump on the spot.

Around the corner and there are Shane and Jason, huddled around the blinding light of an iPhone. Jason looks up and sees Wayne and says, "Get a load of this, Pumphrey," followed by Shane saying, "They're real, too."

Wayne doesn't go over. "Perhaps you ought to turn that off now since the band has started."

Jason nods.

"They're real, too," Shane says again.

Wayne finds Julie and Les near stage right. Les is holding Julie's script. "No, no, no!" he tells her. "You're not giving the words enough emphasis. Try it like this: Oh, *Clancy,* I *never* thought *you'd* come *home*! Hit every second word. And try crying. No, no, no, not like that. Put your hands over your face. Right, that's it. And bend over like you've just been punched. No, that's *too* far over." Les notices Wayne then, and says, "Well if it isn't *Mr. Assistant Director.*"

Julie gets to full height and takes her hands away from her face. "Here to give us some pointers, *Mr. Assistant Director?*"

"No. Just checking in."

"Well that's nice of *Mr. Assistant Director,* isn't it, Julie?"

"Sure is," Julie says. "By the way, how do Marjorie's pants look on me, Wayne? Pretty good, eh?"

"They look better on you than they did on her,"

Les says, licking his fingers and then smoothing his hair.

"The band's well underway," Wayne says, "and places will be called soon and I just wanted to wish you both the best."

"Isn't that sweet of *Mr. Assistant Director?*" says Julie.

"Very," says Les.

Wayne goes to leave, but Julie says, "You'll see how good we are without her."

Les nods. "Don't need Marjorie Pope to get to St. John's."

Wayne lingers a moment and then walks on. Pushes open the door that leads into the corridor. Bright lights and the smell of Lysol and ancient Mr. Ricketts there wringing a mop. The janitor looks up, tries to straighten to full height, but can only make it halfway. He looks like a broken pool stick. Staring over the rim of his bifocals, he says, "They make me mop, but no one'll come this way. Tomorrow you youngsters will traipse through tracking mud everywhere and it'll look like I never did it in the first place and they'll be wanting me to retire, which is fine only how would I spend my days?"

Faintly, Wayne hears the band start in on their second number. No drums or guitar or saxophones, just flutes and French horns and violins and it's the sad song that also closes the show.

"Isn't your play about to start?" Mr. Ricketts says.

"Soon."

Mr. Ricketts nods. Then he holds out his mop. "Want to take over here?"

Wayne smiles. Shakes his head.

"Didn't think so."

The janitor starts mopping again.

"Mr. Ricketts?"

"Hmm?"

"If someone you knew wanted you to go somewhere, would you?"

"Depends."

"On what?"

Mr. Ricketts leans on his mop. "Where we were going. *Who* I was going with. Why do you ask?"

Wayne pauses. "No reason."

Just then the door at the end of the corridor opens and Wayne takes in the too-short jacket and the sneakers with the different-coloured laces and the jeans that don't go past the ankles and the messy hair and the way she's now standing with her hands in her back pockets and her feet crossed.

The janitor looks at her. "Who's that?"

Then Wayne's running and Mr. Ricketts is shouting for him to stop because the floor is wet and who do you think they're going to blame if Wayne falls and breaks his neck.

Marjorie's running too and she and Wayne meet halfway and for a moment it looks like they might hug, but they don't.

"Marjorie!"

"Am I too late?"

"No, there's time."

"Does everyone hate me?"

"Hate you! I think Kendrick might kiss you! Sharon and Mr. Rollie, too!"

"What about you, Wayne Pumphrey? Will you kiss me?"

Everything inside him goes to mush and his face burns and his legs turn to rubber and he forgets to breathe and Marjorie laughs and grabs his wrist and they start running towards the stage door.

"Stop!" Mr. Ricketts screams.

But just then the stage door opens and Mr. Rollie's standing there and he's the colour of bread, but upon seeing Marjorie the blood rushes back into his cheeks. "Miss Pope!"

Wayne and Marjorie stop in front of him.

"Have you come back?" Mr. Rollie says.

"If you'll have me."

Mr. Rollie's holding her suddenly and Marjorie's holding him back and Mr. Ricketts wants to know what in blazes is going on and then the audience applauds and the band starts in on their third and final number before the opening of the show.

Mr. Rollie lets Marjorie go. "We'll have to get Julie out of your pants." Then to Wayne, "We have a situation."

"I'd say," Mr. Ricketts says.

"Situation?" says Wayne.

"Mr. Faulkner."

"Les?"

"He tripped over Mr. Stool who was lying on the floor and he's twisted his knee and it's quite bad and I don't think he can go on."

"No!"

"Yes. So I need you to fill in."

"What?"

"I was all ready to call it off, but then I thought: who has sat in on every rehearsal and helped me rewrite sections of the script and knows everyone's lines? You, Mr. Pumphrey ... *YOU!*"

"Me?" Wayne looks at Marjorie, then back at Mr. Rollie. "But you said I should join the band."

"I made a mistake and I'm sorry and if there's anyone who deserves a chance it's you, Mr. Pumphrey."

Wayne pauses. "What about Paul? Have you asked him?"

"Mr. Stool can't say the one line he *has*, Mr. Pumphrey. No, I've thought this through. There's no one but you."

"But I can't. I'll mess it up."

A flurry of cymbals coming from the stage area; trumpets loud enough to straighten Mr. Ricketts's back; a sound from the flutes that only a dog could hear; and a hand in his suddenly: longish, icicle-like fingers. Then her voice. Older-sounding. Like someone who's seen stuff. "You can do it, Wayne Pumphrey."

He turns to her—to the fatherless girl with the worn sneakers and the funny hair and the strange mother—and believes that, so long as she's doing it with him, he might be able to do it too. Then he looks back at Mr. Rollie. Breathes in and holds it for ages and finally lets it out and says, "I'd like to use a script."

Marjorie's hand is squeezing his now, and Mr. Rollie's jumping up and down and clapping, and Mr. Ricketts is saying, "Fall then, see if I care!"

⌒

They're running: Mr. Rollie up front and Marjorie and Wayne not far behind, through the stage door and into the wings and to the backstage as the drums taper off and the saxophones go quiet and Dean Dunn lets go of his whammy bar, making way, finally, for the clarinets, which sound awkward and self-conscious and a bit flat. Someone's playing the triangle. Jim Butt, Wayne guesses.

Everyone's gathered around Les. Kendrick's holding an ice pack against Les's knee and Julie's massaging Les's shoulders. Sharon's holding a Snickers wrapper and Paul is telling those who will listen that it wasn't his fault and why wasn't Les watching where he was going. Shane and Jason are giggling.

"You were lying in the middle of the floor!" Les shouts.

"You did it on purpose," Julie says.

"Did not."

"Trying to sabotage my performance!" goes Les.

Then Sharon screams, "Marjorie!"

Everyone looks. Some of the younger cast members hold their hands to their mouths.

A cymbal crashes. Dean Dunn does another lick. A crescendo amongst the woodwinds.

Julie's eyes are bulging in their sockets and Les's jaw is on his lap and Kendrick's smiling like a drunk.

"What is *she* doing here?" Julie says.

Mr. Rollie says, "Take off your pants, Miss Snow."

"What?"

"You too, Mr. Faulkner. Mr. Pumphrey has graciously offered to fill in for you."

The cast's communal gasp drowns out the crescendo in the music. Hands go to mouths; others reach out and grab shoulders. Sharon drops her Snickers wrapper and Paul seems to be fighting the

urge to lie down again; Les goes even paler; and
Julie's eyes swell more than Les's knee has. Then Les
is pushing the ice pack aside and telling everyone
he can do the show after all and tries getting to his
feet, but the pain's too much, so Kendrick lowers
him back onto his chair. Les licks his palm and goes
to run it through his show-ready hair, but his heart's
not in it, so instead he looks at Mr. Rollie and says,
"Fill in? Him? He'll ruin everything."

Then the music's ending and the lights are going
down and Mr. Rollie orders Kendrick to run out and
tell Mrs. Cooper to play for a few more minutes and
for the rest of the cast to find their places. Everyone
reaches for personal props and adjusts costume bits
and runs to entrance positions. Sharon's holding
her stomach and Paul's saying something about not
knowing his line. Then the music dies completely
and the curtain starts to open but then Kendrick
reappears and the music starts again and the curtain
closes before too much of the set is revealed and a
bedsheet is held up for Marjorie and Julie to change
behind and Marjorie's costume pants are so short
they look comical and Julie walks to her place like a
mourner following a casket.

Les takes off his flannel shirt, sweater, parka,
work gloves, and hard hat, handing them all over to
Wayne. He refuses to give up the pants though and
insists on Kendrick taking him somewhere where

he doesn't have to listen to all his excellent acting being butchered by Wayne Pumphrey.

Kendrick helps Les to his feet and half carries him away while Wayne gets into Les's clothes that are too big. Marjorie's there to roll up his shirt-sleeves; Mr. Rollie adjusts the hard hat to fit Wayne's head; Jason's placing a script in his hands.

Then he's being guided to his place and his shoulder is squeezed and a voice that's Mr. Rollie's says, "You're a leader."

Marjorie. Where's Marjorie?

An explosion in the music: everything struck or blown into or strummed with full force, and his lips and ears are tingling, and his heart's racing, and he can't breathe, and how'd he end up here anyway? Applause and whistling and stomping of feet that seems to go on forever and then the lights going down and then nothing. He's moving again, but it doesn't feel like *his* feet doing the walking; they're someone else's, pulling his strings, taking him to where he needs to be. Must be. Now he's still, and alone, and he thinks *We all are anyway,* and it's black and he can't see and he fumbles to open the script, find the page, but he drops it and it echoes and then the spotlight heats his face and it's like he's died and is heading towards the light, or rather the light's heading towards him, about to engulf him. *Bend down and pick up the script,* he thinks. Open it up and read. Simple. But he can't move. Can't do anything but stare into the light. And it dawns on him then that mostly everything is out of our hands, so maybe it's just best to get out of the way.

It's the sound of laughter at the back of the gymnasium that brings Wayne back. That and Mr. Rollie whispering the opening line from his place in the wings, and Jim Butt dropping a drumstick, and the people in the front row whispering. *Pick up the script*, he thinks once more, but again he doesn't. Why would he need to when the words are in his head all of a sudden? He doesn't know if they're the right words, only that they're coming from somewhere and they *feel* like the right ones. Almost like how you know what someone's saying without them having spoken; you know by what their body does instead, their eyes, the way they hold their mouths or tuck a strand of hair behind their ear or walk away because that too is saying something. *So many words*, Wayne thinks, *when really, we hardly need them at all.*

Then Marjorie's there and she's addressing the audience and her eyes are glossy and then the lights come up to full and Paul Stool enters from stage left and gives Wayne a hug, which gets a big laugh because the eight-year-old son is bigger than the thirty-year-old daddy. Then Marjorie's hugging Wayne too and kissing him (not in the script, the kissing part) and she mistakenly knocks his hard hat off and it rolls into the wings, which makes the audience laugh again. The action moves to the kitchen and Wayne's character Clancy is telling his wife and son about the accident at the mine and how Roy from across the road is unaccounted for. Lights out and then Mrs. Cooper goes to the piano and the rest of the cast filter onstage for "The Mining Song," which in Wayne's opinion sounds slightly off key. A scene at the mine then: men digging through rubble, and one in a union hall where angry workers demand safer working conditions. Paul Stool forgets his one line and stops blinking and Wayne has to say the words for him. Another song and Julie has a solo and she's not bad despite her slip showing. Then a funeral scene where Sharon (her character's name is Beverly) laments the loss of her husband, Roy. She's doing great until her wig falls off and the audience laughs through the rest of her monologue and into the next scene. Paul Stool trips and knocks over a vase of flowers sitting on the kitchen table in scene nine and then, inexplicably, says the line that he'd forgotten earlier and some in the audience chuckle; others whisper; someone unwraps candy.

Then Wayne and Marjorie are in heavy coats and they're standing on a street corner and Wayne's character Clancy says: "Spring's coming," to which Marjorie's character Bonita replies: "Long way off

yet. Spring." And suddenly Wayne can't remember
what comes next, so he looks into the wings, but
there's no one, so he tries listening for Mr. Rollie's
prompt, but there's no voice. Marjorie's staring and
he's wishing now he'd picked up that script and read
from the page so he wouldn't be lost. He thinks
there's nothing worse: being lost. It's in his mind to
walk offstage, grab a copy of the play, and then come
back out, but he's got no feet, legs, body, brain. He's
hardly there—a breeze. Then Marjorie speaks and it
occurs to him that he couldn't remember because he
had no words to begin with. Her last lines are spoken
directly to the audience and it's something about
wishing she could keep Clancy with her all the time
so she wouldn't have to worry, or hear about him the
way she'd heard about Roy and why do bad things
have to happen? "But time supplies the gauze," Bonita
says, "the bandages and eventually the cast." Then her
character turns to Wayne's character and they hold
hands and walk offstage as the lights go down and the
band starts its instrumental of "The Mining Song."

Applause and the lights up to full and the cast in
a jagged line and bowing at different times because,
in all the chaos of the past few days, Mr. Rollie had
neglected to rehearse a curtain call. Marjorie and
Wayne are pushed to the front, so they grab hands
and bow, and the audience gets to their feet. Then
Mr. Rollie comes out, wiping beneath his glasses,

and saying how happy he is that everyone could make it out and, despite some pre-show hiccups, the performance couldn't have been better and he likes his odds in next week's drama festival, which makes the audience clap even louder.

Everyone leaves the stage, and in the wings there are hugs and handshakes and pats on the back and voices saying "Way to go, Wayne"; "Like you've been doing it all along"; "Better than Les." Then Julie's standing there and she's fanning her dress and she says, "My slip was showing."

"I bet everyone was too focused on your singing to notice," Wayne says.

She pauses. "I was thinking that maybe I don't like this stuff as much as I thought."

Wayne stays quiet.

"Most of the time I'm thinking about skirts and shoes."

"Can't help thinking stuff."

"I suppose." She makes to go, but stops. "You did really good."

"Thanks."

"So did Marjorie. Can you tell her for me? I'd do it myself but I can't find her anywhere."

Wayne nods.

Julie walks away.

"Reception's in room 214," Mr. Rollie says. "But first you should go out and meet your adoring fans."

The place clears out in minutes and Wayne gets back into his civilian clothes and walks onto the stage to have a look in the auditorium.

She's sitting in the fourth row from the front, her hands in her lap.

"There you are," he says.

She looks up.

He goes to where she is. "There's a reception."

"I know."

Wayne sits down beside her. "Wanna go?"

"Rather not."

"But you're the star."

"Go without me."

"Would Leo go without Kate?"

"Pfft."

"What?"

"We're far from Kate and Leo."

"Not tonight."

Marjorie pauses. *"Tonight."*

For ages they sit and say nothing, like people at ease with each other, comfortable in the silence.

Then the door at the back opens and Mr. Ricketts walks in. He stops for a moment and scratches the back of his head, then starts stacking chairs.

Marjorie says, "You were excellent."

"No, you were." Then, "What do you think our chances are next week?"

"Don't know."

"I had a dream about St. John's last night: I was on Signal Hill staring at the ocean and whales were breaching."

It's quiet for a moment.

"Did your mom come?" Wayne says.

"She'd have to wash her hair and get out of her robe for that." Marjorie pauses. "Doesn't matter. Even if she did come, she wouldn't have seen it."

Wayne says, "Why'd you change your mind?"

"I don't know."

"I'm glad you did."

Mr. Ricketts's voice: "Can't stack chairs with bums in 'em."

Wayne looks back. "Can we help?"

"Help? They'd have me in a rocking chair *tonight*!"

A hand on top of his own. He looks down and then across at her.

"Let's go," she says.

"To the reception?"

She shakes her head.

"Where then?"

"You'll see."

They both stand and Marjorie leads him back towards the stage as Mr. Ricketts coughs and mumbles and drops a chair and curses.

In the wings now and to the backstage where she stops and faces him and kisses him and uses her tongue and he thinks her saliva tastes like raisins.

Then she lets him go and guides him to the door leading into the corridor, and when she pulls it open Pete The Meat is there.

# FIVE

Bobby and Harvey are dragging Wayne; Pete's just ahead, holding Marjorie's wrist against her back at an odd angle while his other arm is around her neck and it looks like it hurts but Marjorie's not making a sound; Kenny's pointing towards an open classroom at the end of the hall.

The floor's still wet from where Mr. Ricketts was mopping and Bobby nearly slips and Harvey laughs and Bobby says it's not funny.

Pete turns around and tells them to hurry up and Wayne thinks he's never seen that look on Pete's face before.

Harvey's digging his fingers into Wayne's arm but Wayne hardly feels it, and Bobby's whispering into his ear but Wayne can't make out the words because he still tastes Marjorie's kiss on his lips.

Then they're inside the classroom and Pete

makes Marjorie and Wayne stand against the chalkboard and Kenny closes the door and flicks off the
lights and then stands there with the moon through
the window lighting his face. Bobby goes to take
something out of his pocket and Pete tells him to
leave it. "But," Bobby says, and Pete goes, "Leave it,
I said," so Bobby does.

Pete steps closer and says, "You're missing a nice
reception upstairs. They got them Vienna sausages—
you'd probably like those, Maple Leaf—and pickle
toothpick thingies and egg sandwiches—"

"And Doritos," Bobby says.

"That's right, Bobby," Pete says, "and Doritos."
The Meat smiles and his teeth glisten because of the
moon. "Your faggot drama teacher made a speech
and then got embarrassed when he couldn't find
either of you."

Bobby laughs, but no one laughs along with him.
Then Pete turns to Harvey and asks him what he
thought of the play and Harvey adjusts his position
on the desk he's sitting on and says, "A fuckin' bore."

Pete nods. "Wasn't it?" Then to Wayne, "And
what were they thinking sending Pumphrey out
there?"

Kenny shrugs and Bobby laughs again and Pete
looks right at Wayne and says, "The leading man, eh?
Think that's what you are, Pumphrey?"

"More than you'll ever be," Marjorie says.

Pete doesn't say anything, just nods, and, despite the murk, it's not hard to make out Harvey getting to full height and Bobby standing with his feet shoulder-width apart and Kenny walking forward.

A truck pulls out of the lot, its headlights shining in the window, allowing Wayne to see everything: the whites of Pete's eyes, and the way The Meat's shirt clings to his chest; Harvey's steel-nosed workboots and nicotine-stained fingers; Bobby's half smile with the now perfect fake tooth highlighting the deficiencies of the rest, their plaque and gingivitis, their crowdedness and cavities; Kenny's furtive glance out the window and then the door, then out the window again; and Marjorie's wet bottom lip from where Wayne's own lips had been just moments ago, and her moist eyes even though she's not crying, and the way her palms are pressed flat against each thigh as if needing something to touch.

Then the lights are gone and it's dark again and Pete's got Marjorie pinned up against the chalkboard by the neck and Wayne shouts, "Let her go!" and then Bobby and Harvey have Wayne pinned up against the chalkboard too and Wayne feels cold despite the heat. Then Pete looks over and says, "He shouts again, put a fuckin' eraser in his gob." To which Bobby replies, "Bet he'd like something *else* in his gob," which makes Harvey laugh.

Another vehicle pulls out of the lot, more lights shining in, and Pete tells Kenny to close the fuckin' blinds and Kenny runs over and does it and now it's even darker, just the shapes of things.

No one says anything.

Wayne hears breathing and swallowing and licking of lips and he thinks about that song and being strange and not belonging anywhere and this here's the proof, right?

A voice: Pete's. "Hand it over."

Bobby snickers and fumbles about and hauls something out of his pocket and hands it to Pete.

Wayne looks and can't make it out at first, but then knows exactly what it is, and he says "No," but no one seems to hear him.

And now Pete's waving it in front of Marjorie's face and saying, "Sorry, Maple Leaf, it thawed in Bobby's pocket, so we'll have to go easy."

Harvey and Bobby laugh.

"I figured I'd let you do it yourself, but then I thought: wouldn't it be great if Pumphrey did it for you? Seeing as you like each other so much."

"Do what?" Wayne says, even though he knows exactly what.

Then Bobby says, "But it's so dark, Pete. How will we see?"

"You'll see, Bobby, don't worry, although sometimes it's better to imagine." Pete brings the

wiener to his nose and smells it. "I said you'd get
what was coming, didn't I, Maple Leaf?"

A silence.

Then Marjorie says, "Should I lie on the desk
over there or on the floor or what?"

Pete doesn't answer, so Bobby goes to speak,
but Pete tells him to shut up and turns to Marjorie
and says, "I know what you're tryin' to do, Maple
Leaf."

Marjorie says nothing.

"But it won't work."

Bobby says, "What's she tryin' to do, Pete?"

"Act like it doesn't bother her, that's what. So
we'll get turned off or something and let them go."

After a moment Bobby says, "But we're not
going to let them go, right, Pete?"

"That's right, we're not. Not until Pumphrey
here gives Maple Leaf what she's dyin' for."

No one says anything.

Wayne feels Harvey's grip loosen, and Bobby—
seemingly too wrapped up in breathing and trying to
swallow without the spit—lets him go, and Kenny's
pacing now like someone waiting for results.

"Not man enough to do it yourself, Pete?"
Marjorie says.

And suddenly it's like a cord being yanked out of
something, leaving an unexpected and exacerbated
silence in its wake that Wayne thinks might go on

forever, except that Pete finally manages to speak. "I'll have my go, Maple Leaf, don't worry."

Then Bobby says, "Me too, Pete?"

"Yes, Bobby, you too. And Kenny if he wants."

Kenny doesn't say whether or not he'd like to.

Now Pete's got Marjorie in a bear hug and is carrying her to the back of the room and when Wayne says to put her down, Bobby hits him full force in the stomach. Down Wayne goes and he thinks it funny how easily the tears come compared to how hard it is to breathe. He'll smother, he figures, but then suddenly he's able to draw breath, sucking in great heaps and then wiping the wetness from his cheeks. He looks up and can make out Marjorie, and Pete standing over her waving the wiener as if she were a dog he was teaching a trick to.

"Bring him over, boys," Pete says.

And he's lifted up despite not having regained his wind and he coughs as he's being dragged there. Now he's standing over Marjorie too and Pete's telling her to take off her pants and make it quick 'cause they don't have all fuckin' night.

Marjorie unbuckles and unzips and slides off and Bobby breathes in Wayne's ear and Harvey squeezes Wayne's arm and Kenny goes over and stands guard by the door and Pete's waving that wiener back and forth like he's conducting something, which, Wayne thinks, he sort of is.

"Grannies," Bobby says, pointing at Marjorie and laughing.

"How would you know, dickwad?" Pete says. "Spying on your mommy again?"

"No," Bobby says.

Quiet for a moment.

Pete looks at Marjorie. "The grannies too, Maple Leaf."

But Marjorie won't, so The Meat tells her for the last time, then Marjorie says, "Why don't *you* take them off, Pete?"

Pete stops waving the wiener. "Don't think I won't, Maple Leaf, yours wouldn't be the first I've taken off."

Everyone goes still.

Then Pete squats down and reaches out, but Marjorie grabs his hand and says, "Ever take off a pair that actually *wanted* to come off, Pete? From someone you actually liked and who happened to like you, too?"

Pete holds Marjorie's stare, then yanks his hand away and stands up and says, "That's why Pumphrey's going to take them off. You're not my type, Maple Leaf, probably catch E. coli if I stuck it in you."

"I'll take them off, Pete—"

"No, Bobby," The Meat says. "Let Pumphrey."

*That noise,* Wayne thinks. *What's that noise?* Then suddenly he knows. It's his own heart pounding in his ears, in the soles of his feet, in his groin, in the tips of his fingers, inside his skull. The floor's pulsating because of it, as are the blinds, the pencils, the chalk. A tightness at the back of his neck then as he's forced on his knees beside her. The whites of her eyes match the white of her panties and it occurs to him that the world's unsafe somehow. Then she touches his hand as if to say, *It's okay, Wayne Pumphrey, it will soon be done,* but he knows it's not okay and it will never be done and where can you go to be safe if you can't be safe at school?

Now she guides his fingers to the band of her underwear and he lets her and then Harvey makes a grunting sound and Pete says to keep going because Marjorie's dying for it and Bobby repeats, "Dying for it."

Voices from the parking lot, opened and closed doors, turned ignitions and pumped gas pedals, engines fading into the night, and the quiet. Always that. And he feels the heat in his fingers, the beginnings of her pubic hair and it's coarse and he thinks he wasn't expecting that.

"Thatta boy, Pumphrey," goes The Meat.

Someone clears his throat. Licks his lips. Swallows. He himself, Wayne realizes. Then he takes his hand away and Pete asks him what he's doing but Wayne won't answer, reaching instead for Marjorie's pants and covering her.

Bobby groans and Pete gets to his knees and grips Wayne by the back of the neck and squeezes, but Wayne doesn't make a sound.

"I was doing you a favour, Pumphrey," Pete says, "but if you won't do it, I know someone who will." Pete lifts his head and looks at Bobby.

"Me?" Bobby says.

"That's right."

But Bobby doesn't move.

"Don't just stand there, dickwad."

Still Bobby won't go over.

Pete shakes his head and says, "All your talk earlier, and now here you are more chickenshit than Pumphrey."

"I'm not chicken," Bobby says.

"No?"

Bobby shakes his head.

"Well get your ass over here then. It's not every day *you* see the real thing."

"Quit it."

"Who said that?" Pete wants to know.

Kenny steps forward. "'Have some fun with them,' you said."

"This *is* fun," Pete says. Then to Bobby, "Isn't it?"

Bobby nods.

"Harvey?" The Meat goes.

Harvey nods too. "She's shown it to hundreds, Kenny."

"That's right, Harvey," Pete says. "Like eating breakfast for Maple Leaf, this is."

"What if someone comes?" Kenny says.

"No one's coming, Kenny," says Pete.

"Yeah, Kenny," Bobby says.

Harvey goes, "Relax."

Kenny seems to be considering it. Then he says, "We could get in trouble."

"What trouble?" says Pete.

"Yeah, what trouble?" repeats Bobby.

"There's no trouble," Harvey says.

Kenny steps back and grips the doorknob but doesn't leave.

"Way to be, Kenny," Bobby says.

"This'll all be over before you know it," Pete says. Then, "Come on Bobby, we don't have all fuckin' night."

Bobby moves in Marjorie's direction.

"NOT ... ANOTHER ... STEP," Wayne says.

Bobby stops.

Pete squeezes Wayne's neck hard and says, "Who do you think you are, Pumphrey! Huh? You're *nothing*, remember, so you got no say in what Bobby does."

Wayne tries to get out of Pete's grip but how can he when Pete's fingers are like steel?

Then a voice from the floor, and it's Marjorie's, and she says, "Leave him alone!"

Pete lets him go and reaches out and covers Marjorie's mouth. "Shut your gob, Maple Leaf." Then to Bobby, "Get over here and hold Pumphrey."

Before Wayne can get to his feet, Bobby's got him around the neck and Wayne can barely breathe and Pete's on top of Marjorie bearing all his weight down with his hand still over her mouth, but Marjorie's fighting back now—kicking and bucking her hips.

And then Harvey's there, giving Pete a hand. Then Kenny. But Kenny's not helping. Trying to haul Harvey off and there's a struggle and a tussle of bodies and the wiener that Pete's been managing to keep hold of goes flying and lands somewhere. And Wayne's suffocating; does Bobby have any idea how hard he's squeezing? Suddenly Harvey's on top of Kenny and he's punching him in the face and it sounds nothing like the movies, Wayne thinks— quieter, more hollow-sounding, like a foot pounding earth. And Marjorie's still struggling beneath Pete, but she manages to bite The Meat's face and Pete hauls back and punches her so hard in the nose that the sound implants itself into everyone's skin and bones and into each organ and there's no way, Wayne thinks, any of them will ever forget it.

There's blood running down The Meat's chin, dripping onto his Adam's apple. He gets off Marjorie. She's holding her face.

Harvey stops punching Kenny. Kenny's lip is cut.

Bobby lets Wayne go and Wayne crawls over to Marjorie and blood's pouring from her nose and he turns to Pete and screams, *"LOOK WHAT YOU DID!"*

Pete doesn't say a word, just kneels there.

Wayne takes off his outer shirt and bunches it up and places it over Marjorie's nose, then he hears a voice he doesn't recognize and when he looks it's Pete and the reason he couldn't place it is because The Meat's crying as he talks and it's strange because he's got that almost-a-moustache and those muscles and yet he sounds like a youngster and Wayne's never seen him cry before and Pete's saying he didn't mean it and why did she bite him in the first place and why did Wayne come to his house and sometimes he doesn't know why he does the things he does.

Then a door opens and lights are flicked on and everyone, save for Pete, looks and sees Mr. Ricketts standing there.

Mr. Ricketts's jaw goes slack. He might faint. Why can't he move past the door?

Wayne's helping Marjorie back into her pants and Bobby's saying "Sorry" over and over and Kenny holds his own lip and Harvey's breathing heavy because all that punching has exhausted him, and Pete ... Pete's still crying.

Finally Mr. Ricketts *is* able to move, going over to where Marjorie and Wayne are and kneeling.

Wayne buckles Marjorie's pants and "Who's responsible?" Mr. Ricketts wants to know.

Then Marjorie's getting to her feet and Mr. Ricketts says she should stay lying, but she ignores him and heads to the door and Wayne follows her.

"What happened here?" Mr. Ricketts says.

But Wayne doesn't answer, leaving the janitor there on his knees surrounded by a placating Bobby and a breathing Harvey and a fat-lipped Kenny and a screeching Pete. Screeches so loud that Wayne can still hear them in the corridor and through the main doors and out into the night.

# SIX

They're standing just beyond school property: Marjorie with her head tilted back and Wayne—still using his shirt—pinching the bridge of her nose. Blood's on her teeth, lips, chin.

He watches her, then looks away. Pete's punch comes to his mind and he almost loses his breath.

She pushes his hand away and lowers her head and blood pools near the opening of one nostril, which she wipes away with her fingertips.

He offers his shirt but she won't take it.

Ages pass.

"He hit you so hard," Wayne says.

She stays quiet.

"Bobby was choking me, otherwise I'd have done more."

Still quiet.

She looks past his shoulder and, from far off, a train's whistle seeps into the night, then dies away.

It takes forever, but finally she turns to face him again. Breathes deep and says, "I'd have taken that tonight, Wayne Pumphrey, if not for you."

Holding her hand's on his mind, but he resists the urge and says nothing.

"You know what you are?" Marjorie says. "Hmm?" Wayne doesn't know.

"A black hole. Sucking everyone into your misery."

Marjorie walks away and Wayne follows and she doesn't get very far before she stops and sits on the sidewalk and puts her face in her hands. Wayne sits beside her and thinks of something to say, but there's nothing. So he waits and waits and finally she takes her hands away and her eyes are sparkling under the glow of the streetlight and there's snot and blood above her top lip, which she wipes on the sleeve of her jacket. "You're just a creep with no friends, Wayne Pumphrey. You're too small and your dad can't drive on the right side of the street. And me—I'm a spaz who sticks wieners in herself and has a dead father and a mother who may as well be, and that's how people are always going to see us, and if you don't know that by now you're stupider than I thought." She stands up and goes to leave but stops herself and when she tries to speak her voice

catches, which brings Wayne forward, but she sticks
her hand out as if to say *Stay where you're to,* so Wayne
does. She tries again and this time words come.
"Pete'll never be gone and we'll always be who we
are and that's just the way it is."

Then a car drives by and slows down and stops
and a window is lowered and a voice says: "Weren't
you two in that play?" Wayne nods and the person
says, "Some job ya did," and then, "Everything okay
here?" And Wayne nods, so the person drives away.

A long silence.

At last Marjorie speaks. "I'd prefer to walk the
rest of the way on my own."

"I don't mind."

"I *DO,* okay!"

Wayne's about to say something, but Marjorie
cuts him off. "Before you, I was mostly left alone.
Yes, they talked about me behind my back and
spread rumours and shit, but no one ever did what
they did tonight."

Wayne stays quiet.

"From now on walk your own self to school,
and if it's cold I won't be needing your jacket
'cause I'll wear an extra layer, and if I happen to
slip because of my sneakers I won't be needing you
to help me up. Just leave me alone, all right! We'll
both be better off anyway." She holds his gaze for a
moment and then turns to walk away and then his

hand's gripping her shoulder and he's wondering how it got there.

"What?" she says.

"I don't know."

"Let go."

"No."

"Let GO!"

He does.

She turns around and walks away.

Wayne doesn't follow.

Then he drops his shirt into the snow.

# SEVEN

They're all waiting in the foyer when Wayne arrives
home. His mother comes over and gives him a hug
and won't let go and his dad comes over too and
messes his hair and Wanda says, "Sure I didn't know
you could act." Then they're dragging him into the
kitchen and sitting him at the table and Wanda grabs
him a Diet Coke, which fizzes when she opens it,
and they're asking him why he didn't come to the
nice reception because they were all waiting.

He goes to stand up.

"Don't want to sit with us?" his mother says.

He sits back down.

Wanda takes her earphones out. "Lap it up while
you can, little brother."

His dad says, "I was sitting there and then the
lights came up and it was you and I leaned over and
said to your mother, 'That's Wayne,' and she goes,

'Yes,' and I says, 'I thought he was behind the scenes,' and your mother says, 'Shush, I can't hear.'"

"Then you dropped your script," Wanda says, "and I'm like, Uh oh, but then you went on like you've been at it all your life. And you know Vanessa Prescott ... big lesbo chick with the pierced nipple?"

"Wanda!"

"What?" Then, "Anyway, she's sitting right beside me and she taps my shoulder and says, 'Little twat's not bad—'"

"Wanda!"

"Well that's what she said, Mom. So I say back, 'No, he isn't, is he?'"

"And that girl from up the road," Wayne's mother says. "The one you brought to Woolworths."

"Marjorie," Wanda says.

"Yes—her ... she was something else. Twice her age it seemed like."

"How did she make herself cry?" Wanda wants to know.

Wayne doesn't answer, so Wanda says, "The thought of kissing you, probably."

Then it's quiet and Wanda goes, "Sure look at the long face on him."

Now everyone's watching and Wayne pushes out his chair and stands up and his mother says, "You don't seem very excited," and his dad says, "What's wrong?," and Wanda, because his jacket's open, says, "What happened to your shirt?"

Wayne just stands there, his palms flat on the table.

"The nice button-up one? Weren't you wearing it earlier?"

Wayne goes to leave but ends up staying where he is. Then Wanda grabs his Diet Coke since he's not drinking it and takes a sip and doesn't give it back.

"It's stupid," Wayne says.

"What's stupid?" says his mother.

"Wanting to be in front of people."

No one has anything to say about that.

"Better off keeping to myself and who needs friends anyway."

His parents exchange glances and Wanda takes another sip of Diet Coke and the grandfather clock strikes ten and then there's a racket on the roof and against the windows, which Wayne thinks must be hail because nice weather never lasts long in Canning.

Someone's at the door and his father goes and answers it and Wayne hears him say, "What happened to you?" and "*Who* do you want—Wayne?" Then his dad comes back in and steps aside and Kenny's there.

Wayne's mother takes in Kenny's swollen lip with the dried blood and the glassy eyes.

Wanda looks at Wayne, then back at Kenny, and says, "What's all this about, little brother?"

Wayne can't speak.

His father pulls out a chair and points to it for Kenny to sit on, but Kenny shakes his head and says he can't stay and would prefer to stand.

"Well, come in at least," Wayne's mother says. "You're half-frozen."

Kenny steps into the kitchen. He's shaking.

"Put the kettle on, Wanda," Wayne's mother says.

Wanda goes over and fills the kettle and puts it on the burner, then leans against the counter and keeps her eyes on Kenny.

"What happened to your face?" Wayne's dad wants to know.

Kenny goes to speak, but Wayne does first. "Can I talk with him alone?"

"Alone?" his father says.

"Why do you need to be alone?" says his mother.

Wanda says, "Were you picking on my brother?"

Kenny doesn't answer and Wayne asks again if he can talk with Kenny alone and his father says, "You'd better tell us what happened tonight," and Wayne says, "I will, but right now I need to speak with Kenny please."

His dad pauses. "Pete The Meat have anything to do with this?"

"Who?" Wayne's mother wants to know. "*Pete The Meat*, did you say?"

"I'll explain later," Wayne says.

Wanda goes, "If you were picking on my brother, then you deserved what you got." She looks at Wayne. "Did *you* do that, little brother? 'Cause right on, if you did."

"Okay," says Wayne's father, "we'll give you a few minutes, but you'd better tell me because I thought we'd dealt with this." He waves to Wanda and his wife. "Come on, you two."

"Was someone picking on you, Wayne?" his mother says.

"He'll tell us later," Wayne's father says, guiding them into the living room.

"But the kettle's about to boil."

"Boy can make his own tea."

His parents and sister round the corner and are heard talking for a moment before going quiet.

Wayne looks at Kenny and Kenny goes back into the foyer, so Wayne joins him.

They're standing just in front of the door.

Kenny's nose is running. He wipes it on his sleeve. "How is she?" he whispers.

"How do you think?"

Kenny puts his hands in his pockets. Avoids Wayne's eyes. "Pete took off. That old janitor guy

tried to stop him, but Pete's fast. I split, too. Not
Bobby and Harvey though, I don't think."

"Why are you here?"

"If I'd known, I never would have helped." Kenny
swallows. "It was supposed to be a laugh."

"Some laugh."

"You don't understand."

"Guess not."

"He has this way about him. It's like you can't
say no."

Wayne doesn't speak.

"He was humiliated that day you mentioned his
real dad and him having a tough start and everything."

"*He* was!"

"Pete freaks."

"*I* freak too ... when I'm locked in a trunk."

Silence.

Kenny says, "Pete's mom told me stuff."

"What stuff?"

"About before his real dad left—"

"What stuff?"

"'You never forget,' she said."

"Forget what?"

"Even if you were a kid."

"Tell me."

"The bad things. You never forget the bad things.
They stay inside and torment you." For the first time,
Kenny looks at him. "What we did was assault."

"Yeah."

"She'll press charges."

"Probably."

"I'll go to jail."

"Good."

"I tried to help."

"Could have helped sooner."

"I know—"

"Before you dragged us down the hall and put us in that classroom and made her strip down—"

"I'm sorry—"

"Don't tell *me*—"

"As if *she'd* listen."

Silence.

"You know none of this would have happened if she hadn't defended you that time."

"So it's my fault?"

"No."

"Go now—"

"You never fought back."

"What?"

"I kept waiting for you to. So Pete would just kick the shit outta you, and then it would be over, but you never did. It became like a game: what new low would Pumphrey submit himself to today." He pauses, using his tongue to survey the gash on his lip, then says, "I suppose I could have spoke up, but I guess I was scared of Pete too."

Neither speaks for a long time.

Kenny grabs the door handle. "I'd take it all back if I could, Pumphrey." He goes to leave but Wayne says,

"You'll never know what it's like to eat yellow snow and be tripped and have pictures taped to your locker and be afraid. You'll never know."

The kettle whistles.

Kenny's holding the door still.

His mom's voice: "It's boiled!"

Kenny nods and chews the insides of his cheeks and blinks something away, then opens the door and leaves.

Wayne watches him go.

His mother's voice again: "Wayne! Did you hear me?"

"I heard you!" he says back. But he doesn't leave the foyer. And if not for his mom coming back into the kitchen and turning off the element her own self, he'd have let the kettle boil dry.

—

He wakes sometime later and thinks she's sitting beside him, so he sits up and looks more closely, but she isn't.

It's sweltering so he kicks off the sheets and goes over to the window and looks out and there's a sliver of moon and some stars but mostly it's just the big cloud from the mine.

He sees her standing there with crossed ankles and wearing her costume from the show and he thinks it strange that she would be. Her nose is still bleeding, but it's much worse, all over her, a pool of it at her feet turning the snow red, so he slides open the window and sticks his head out and goes to speak but no one's there so he stays quiet.

Closing the window now and he's having trouble breathing and his eyes are wet and his nose is running and he's making a mess on the window, but he wipes it away and rubs his hand on his pyjama pants and goes back over to his bed and lies down and stares at the ceiling.

And his hand is wandering just beneath her panties again and he can feel the prickliness on his fingertips and how fast his heart was beating and how, despite everything, a part of him enjoyed it.

He gets up again and goes over to his desk and sits down and switches on the tiny lamp. Pulls open the drawer and takes out his notebook and a Razor Point extra-fine pen and finds a page.

Dear Marjorie,

Did you mean what you said that I'm a black hole and I suck everyone into my ~~meis~~ misery? What about when you said we're better off staying away from each other? Did you mean that too? But we're creeps, aren't we, and we don't fit in here so we're connected, right?

I'd love to take the train with you but I'm not brave and how would we eat and how do you make a beaded necklace anyway?

Kenny saved you tonight but I wanted it to be me and now you'll never see me as the saving kind, will you?

I thought I saw you sitting on my bed earlier. Then out the window when I looked. I had the strangest feeling. Then I started crying and I didn't even know it until it was happening and I hope it didn't wake Mom because she's a light sleeper.

Will you come back to school? I hope so because what would Mr. Rollie do without his leading lady? And aren't you dying to know what will happen at the drama festival? Can you imagine if we won? Imagine ... George Street and the Avalon Mall and Signal Hill and the smell of the ocean and The Irish Descendants and no one knowing us or gawking and wouldn't you love that? We'd get away from here, Marjorie! AT LAST!! Only for a while, but still that's something, right? RIGHT???

There's one more thing and I feel awful about it but I sort of liked tonight. Not them taking us or anything, and certainly not the punch, but when I was touching you down there I mean, and it was like touching the clouds or a smooth stone and you'd think a guy who

writes so many letters would be able to describe it
better, but I can't. I've never touched a girl, Marjorie, or
even kissed one until tonight. You're my friend yes, but I
think I love you too and I wish you did me, but I know
people rarely feel the same about each other. I think
my mom loves my dad more. Who loved who more
when your dad was alive?

Has your nose stopped bleeding? If I was there I'd
make sure your head was tilted back and I'd offer you
my pyjama top, all my shirts if you wanted, and then
I'd stare at your long neck and think about kissing that
too.

Your friend who loves you,
Wayne Pumphrey

He closes his notebook and switches out the light
and, for the longest time, sits there in the dark.
Then he goes back to bed and curls into a ball and
falls asleep.

He dreams of sirens.

# EIGHT

Wayne's staring at his Honeycombs while Wanda
smears peanut butter on toast and then jabs a straw
into her Diet Coke. She looks up and says, "I can't
believe you slept through those sirens."

The cereal's soggy, so he lifts the bowl and drinks
the milk, leaving the Honeycombs. Pushes the bowl
aside. "I figured I was dreaming."

"Those sirens weren't a dream. A fire, I thought,
but there wasn't any smoke."

He watches her indented cheeks and the stream
of Diet Coke travelling up the straw and into her
mouth, and her swallowing and her watery eyes
because it burns going down, especially at seven-
thirty in the morning.

Enough wind to carry the house away.

They listen to it.

Then Wayne says, "Wonder what happened."

His sister licks peanut butter from the corner of her mouth. "Some bagboy at Dominion lost his shit and started shooting, probably."

*"Here?"*

"Why not *here?*"

Wayne pauses. "A bear roaming the dump, I'd say."

"Yeah, right, every cop car in Canning sent out for a stupid bear."

The grandfather clock chimes.

"It must have been serious though, whatever it was," Wanda says. "Turn on the radio."

Wayne gets up and flicks it on, then comes back over and sits down.

They listen to a story about a three-legged cancer-sniffing dog named Conrad and about a new bingo hall that's going up and the weather report that's calling for more unusually mild temperatures and high winds and, later in the day, wet snow. Nothing about the sirens.

Footsteps in the hall and a closed door.

"You won't go to hell if you miss a day, you know," Wanda says. "Not like you don't have a good excuse."

Wayne thinks of Marjorie: the whiteness of her underwear, the punch, the blood that wouldn't stop, the train she wanted to take. He goes to speak but can't get it out, so he tries again. "I wanted to do more, you know. For Marjorie, I mean."

His sister looks at him. "Did what you could, I'd say. She's lucky you were there."

Wayne shakes his head and says, "But none of it would have happened if not for me."

"No."

"It's true."

His sister looks away.

A toilet flushes.

"She thinks we're better off not hanging out."

"What?"

"I shouldn't bother loaning her my jacket anymore, she said, or helping her up if she slips because I'm a black hole."

"What?"

"Never mind—"

"Black hole, did you say?"

The door opening now. Approaching footsteps.

"She's angry," Wanda says. "Give her time."

Wayne thinks he might like to take the train after all.

Then his mother's there and she's asking if he heard the sirens and Wanda says he dreamed them, only that it wasn't a dream, and then his mother kisses his cheek and says it's no wonder he slept through them … everything he's been through.

A few moments later his dad is taking the kettle off the burner and telling Wayne about the sirens and not to bother with school today or for the rest of the week as far as he's concerned, but Wayne says Mr. Rollie's giving notes on last night's perform- ance so it'd be best if he went.

His father nods and pours tea and grabs a molasses bun and goes over and tells Wanda to get out of his spot so he can sit down before work.

Now they're all sitting and listening to the radio and his mother looks at Wayne and says, "It's not Tuesday, but come to Woolworths for lunch anyway."

Wayne shrugs.

"Half fries and half onion rings. How does that sound?"

He doesn't answer, getting to his feet instead, and everyone seems about to say something but no one does, so he goes into the foyer and gets into his jacket and boots. On his way to the door a news bulletin comes on the radio and there's someone in Burgess Lake that's drowned and they're looking for the body and Wayne's mother says, "Oh my God!" and his father says, "Isn't that terrible," and his sister goes, "That explains the sirens," and Wayne pushes open the door and starts running down the porch steps.

# NINE

Marjorie's mother opens the door and her face is red and her eyes remind Wayne of his father's after a night of Bacardi Dark. She steps out onto the porch and grabs his shoulders and shakes him and says, "Where is she?"

Wayne gets out of her grip and steps back. "I don't know."

Mrs. Pope moans like she's in pain and rubs her face, then takes her hands away. "She didn't come home last night."

Something at the bottom of his belly … like emptiness without the hunger, like waking up in the middle of the night to his father's stumbling and knocking things over. He turns around, half expecting to see Marjorie there, but she isn't, so he faces front again.

Marjorie's mother reaches back and grips the doorknob and Wayne thinks it's so she won't fall down, and the wind messes her hair and blows open her robe exposing the nightgown and the sagging breasts underneath. She lets go of the door and ties a bow in the waist of her robe and grips the knob again and says, "Those awful sirens last night, and when I called the police they told me there was an emergency and when I asked if it was my Marjorie they said they couldn't say. 'I have a right to know,' I said, and they said it was too soon, but they'd take my number and a description and call me once they knew."

Wayne tries to make sense of her words, thinking that he too may need the doorknob to hold, or the banister, or the older lady's shoulders ... *anything*.

Suddenly Mrs. Pope slams the door and Wayne jumps in fright. Then she opens it and slams it again and again and one more time until her neighbour comes out and asks what the ruckus is about and Marjorie's mother screams and tells her to mind her own Jesus business.

The neighbour goes back inside and Wayne wishes he'd had the guts to have grabbed her daughter's hands and looked into her eyes and agreed to pack a bag and hop on a boxcar and get clear of this fucking place forever, but now it's too late because he's sure something bad has happened, as sure as he's standing on her porch, which is probably one of the last places she stood or will *ever* stand.

Now he's taking the steps two at a time, and Marjorie's mother continues to grip the doorknob and shout into the wind for him to come back because he *must* know where she is.

—

And he's running. Always running, except now he's unsure if it's *to* something or *away* from something. And the wind's pushing against him and he thinks it's like another kind of bully.

He makes a right at Balsam Street and picks up the pace and stumbles but rights himself, then runs even harder to escape the loneliness and imagines her hands and crossed ankles and too-short jeans and jacket, and he thinks about the sirens and could they possibly have been for her? *You know what you are? Hmm? A black hole sucking everyone into your misery.*

Boots against the pavement and the wind and his clenched fists and he can't get his head around being here one minute and then not the next.

A vehicle whips past. Then two boys are running beside him and he knows they're brothers and that they go to the other school because they're Jehovah's Witnesses and their mother dresses like

Laura Ingalls and rings people's doorbells and hands
out pamphlets.

And it isn't long before Wayne notices other
people running and cars and trucks either parked or
parking along the curb; some of the bigger vehicles
have their wheels half on the sidewalk.

He's afraid to ask, so he doesn't, just follows the
brothers to the end of Gower Street, then down
the hill to Burgess Lake, which is where everyone
swims for the one week in late August. The brothers
keep going, but Wayne slows down, then stops
altogether. And his sister was right: those sirens
weren't a dream, because how can an ambulance
and a bunch of police cars and a fire truck all parked
at the lip of the lake be a dream?

Now he's looking out and there are boats and
people in them looking over the sides into the icy
water as if at their own reflections. A man holds
a megaphone and someone in scuba gear falls
backwards into the lake and so does another one
in another boat. And the wind is tossing everything
and rippling the water and the people inside the
boats have to hold on tight.

The shore is loaded with people, everyone in
Canning it looks like. They're staring at the water
and the man holding the megaphone. Save for
blowing hair and flapping open jackets, they're still,
even the children—most of whom are hugging their

dad's legs or burying their faces into their mother's hips.

Wayne's chest hurts or maybe it's his heart inside it that hurts, and his ears are ringing and he wants to turn around and run back up the hill but he can't. So he walks forward, slowly, like someone out of options.

He finds a spot at the back and listens to the mumblings being lifted and carried on the wind. He hears "Body in the water," and "Only a youngster," and "Awful isn't it, drowning?" and "Poor thing," and some child says: "Are they in heaven now?," and another, older-sounding one says: "Not if it was suicide," to which a woman's voice goes: "Hush, you two—"

And he imagines her beneath the grimy water with its pop cans and beer bottles and chip bags and old tires and her eyes are open and he wonders why he'd picture them that way, or why he has her smiling too, as if to say: *Stick a wiener in this!*

Suddenly there's a commotion in one of the boats that has nothing to do with the wind and the man with the megaphone is shouting to the other boat to come on over because a scuba diver has resurfaced and is waving his arms like a drowning person.

And a hush falls over the crowd and some palms go to mouths and some arms are draped across backs and some fingers are intertwined and some heads bury themselves into chests and shoulders and armpits and somewhere there's crying or maybe it's just the wind.

The other boat goes over and the second scuba diver comes to the surface and has something in his arms and it looks to Wayne like a head and neck and some torso but he's too far away to be sure.

A gasp.

Someone has to be lowered onto their bum because they're almost fainting.

A child laughs and is told to quiet down, then laughs again, and Wayne can't move. Can't look away either, although he'd like to. And the wind picks up and the sky's spitting despite the weather guy having said that the wet snow wouldn't come until this evening.

The body is lifted from the water and is laid beside the megaphone guy and someone near the stern pulls the motor cord and steers the boat towards land but it's hard going with all the ice.

Maybe it's Wayne's imagination, but everyone on shore seems to take a communal step backward as if uneasy with death's approach. Uneasy, yet at the same time longing to look because we're all going to be a body in a boat.

He forces his eyes away and, in the distance, sees the blowing red hair that's like fire and the glasses and the hand with the pinky ring over a mouth and it's Mr. Rollie and Wayne wants to run over and stand beside him just to stand beside him, but he stays where he is and wonders instead if his drama teacher is thinking what he himself is: that Marjorie's in that boat, Marjorie with the thin fingers and the calling and the acting that's better than the Hollywood crowd and now she'll be with her father and it shouldn't be much longer before her mother decides to join them, too.

Mr. Rollie looks away because the boats are there and two police officers are wet up to the waist trying to drag them ashore.

"SPACE!" the megaphone guy shouts. "For God's sake, give us *SPACE!*" but no one moves because how are you supposed to when nothing makes sense?

Now the officers and the scuba divers and the paramedics are gathered around the boat with the body and someone says to take the head and another says to take the legs and another says to take it easy, but a bunch disagree, saying that this *isn't* the time to take it easy.

Wayne pushes his way through the crowd and some step aside and others don't, and some say that it's rude of him to want to get to the front just so he can gawk, but it's not about gawking so much as it's about needing to see his only friend that's dead and lying there and only last night the lights had been shining on them both and her eyes were alive and glistening so how could they not be *now*?

He gets to the front, but officers are there with outstretched arms and they're keeping everyone back, so Wayne looks past them and sees the paramedics on their knees and one's breathing into Marjorie's mouth and the other is pumping her chest and counting and a fireman holds his helmet next to his chest and wipes his eyes because he's probably thinking of his own little girl and then the wet snow comes hard and fast but no one moves because wet snow means nothing compared to this. And then there's a voice in the distance and he turns around and it's Marjorie's mother running down the hill towards the lake and she's still in her robe.

Wayne focuses back on the paramedics who are now looking at each other, bowing their heads, wiping the wet from their faces or is it tears and getting to their feet and walking away and the body is there for everyone to see and Wayne loses his breath and nearly falls because it's not Marjorie.

# TEN

Dear God or whoever,

How can our lungs be drawing breath and our hearts pumping blood and our brains thinking thoughts and then have it all stop like a wound-down toy and if it's really you or whoever that's in charge then you're either stupid or else you didn't think things through when you started everything!

It didn't look real, more like plastic or rubber or something and I can't believe that's what we look like when the life's gone. They carried the body right by me and I looked away and covered my mouth as if it was contagious but then it dawned on me that I have it already so what's the point?

Why all the wet snow? Were you meaning to wash it away?

What a waste some lady said and when I looked she was shaking her head and looking into her purse

and pulling out a stick of gum and unwrapping it and
then putting it back without chewing it and someone
laughed and a fight broke out and the cops had to hold
a man down and then some kid pulled down his pants
and just started peeing and I wonder if that's what they
call shock?

And there I was thinking that it was sort of what I
wanted but not REALLY so am I partway responsible?

I thought it was her, so I imagined walking into
the water my own self 'cause what did you think I
would do without my fellow creep? But it wasn't, it was
someone else.

Will they cancel school tomorrow? What about the
drama festival? It's the last thing I should be thinking
about, I know, but I'd rather think of that than what I
saw today.

Can you bring the life back? Probably not, eh. I
mean, if you don't do it for little babies you certainly
won't for a fifteen-year-old.

Your friend who knows you can't bring the life back,
Wayne Pumphrey

# ELEVEN

All the pews are full, so people have to stand near the back. Some are holding babies, while others fan themselves with their programs because it's warm with everyone jammed in. It smells of perfume and old wood, and hardly a moment goes by without a child's whining or a blown nose or a cough or a sneeze.

Wayne sits in the centre right aisle, Wanda and his mother on one side of him and his father on the other. Wearing his good trousers and hardly worn shoes and his tie's a clip-on and his shirt's too big around the neck. Hair gelled and parted to the side and he's splashed on some of his dad's aftershave.

The casket is just in front of the altar, yellow-flower bouquets on either side, a framed photograph resting on a mahogany table: Pete in track pants and holding dumbbells and there's sweat on his forehead and he's looking right at the camera and his face seems to be saying *No pain, no gain,* and behind him, on the wall, is a UFC poster of welterweight champion Georges St-Pierre.

What was that the priest just said ... something about being taken before your time but having left an impression anyway? *I'd say,* Wayne thinks.

Pete's mom wails and Pete's second dad goes to hold her but she pushes him away, so he tries again and this time she lets him, burying her face in his chest.

The priest adjusts the mike and moves his mouth closer and tells everyone that God will bear the grief, but Wayne doesn't think that's likely. That's when he sees her, two rows ahead, on the left side. Hair done up and wearing a dress, and her mother's beside her. Out from behind the curtains at last. Marjorie must sense him staring because she looks back and their eyes meet and he tries to smile or lift his brows in acknowledgment but he's frozen, so she turns back around.

Then the priest leaves the pulpit and a member of the congregation walks up and takes his place and it's Mr. Avery and he fumbles in his pocket and pulls out a piece of paper, but drops it and doesn't pick it up. Grips each end of the pulpit and goes to speak but nothing comes, so he lowers his head, then raises it and tries again. And it's all about Peter as a boy. The way he'd sit in the middle of the kitchen and play trucks for hours and how he could never get enough of his mother's cod au gratin. How, when he was older, he made snow forts and skated on the homemade rink till the sun went down and it was freezing. Then came the two and a half hours of weightlifting every night and the raw eggs in a glass and the jogging and the skipping rope and the obsession with the UFC. Mr. Avery pauses to clear his throat and to wipe his forehead. Another deep breath and now it's about how Peter's real dad hadn't treated him right and how Peter had his challenges and wasn't a saint and got into trouble but was loved more than anything and Pete's second dad says that he was blessed to have had what time he did with his son.

Mr. Avery stops and looks at the casket for a long time, then he turns back and presses his lips against the mike and says, "Hug your kids tonight." He steps away from the pulpit as the organ kicks in and the choir starts "Amazing Grace" and the rest of Pete's family filter up to say their goodbyes. Mr. Avery stumbles en route and Pete's mom bumps into the casket. Another man who looks a lot like Pete's second father drapes his arm across her back and steadies her. There are others too: a youngish woman with short hair and fat thighs, and two skinny teenage boys not much older than Wayne. They stand

in front of the casket for so long that the choir starts
"Amazing Grace" again. Pete's mother is the first
to walk away, but she doesn't seem to know where
she's going and the man who looks like Mr. Avery
goes over and takes her hand and shows her. Mr.
Avery has gone pale and looks exhausted and seems
to be sweating as he struggles to make the few steps
back to his seat. The rest wait patiently behind him.
After they're seated, others go up. One boy peers
into the casket for so long the priest has to tell him
to move on. Two girls who might be sisters walk up
arm in arm, but neither can find the courage to look
inside. Mr. Rollie goes up and Adrian's with him and
he has long hair and a week's work of stubble on
his chin. Then the principal's there and Mrs. Cooper
and the geography teacher and Mr. Ricketts and his
ancient-looking wife, Daphne, who's even more
hunched over than her husband. Then more people.
And more still. The organist has to stop to shake
out her cramping fingers. She plays again. Then
Bobby's there, and he places his palms on the casket
and bends over, seemingly getting ready to crawl in
himself—to join his friend in the afterlife so they
can bully the angels—but his father is there to grip
his shoulder and keep him in the land of the living.
Harvey's next, walking up with his parents and his
hair's all cut and he's wearing a nice suit and shoes
and he looks like he's lost weight.

Wayne's father nudges him and whispers, "You don't have to," but Wayne says he wants to. And when he looks towards the front again, Marjorie is just getting there. Her mother isn't with her and she waits for the person ahead of her and then goes up herself and looks at Pete for ages. Now his own mother's lips are against his ear. "Isn't that her?" she says. Wayne nods and then Wanda leans over and says, "It's a wonder *she's* here." Wayne looks up and Marjorie's still there and people are waiting but she stays where she is. Now the priest's going over and he places a hand on her shoulder and says something in her ear and you can see Marjorie nodding but still she doesn't move. And the choir starts "Amazing Grace" for the third time and suddenly Wayne's on his feet and his father tells him it's not his turn yet but Wayne ignores him and pushes past the others in the pew and goes out into the centre aisle and starts walking. He slips past those in line, up to Marjorie and the priest and goes to speak but he's too taken aback by the look of Pete to get the words out: his almost-a-moustache shaved off and so white and looking nothing like himself, more wax than human, and Wayne wonders if it's all some joke and where's the real Pete? Then the priest's asking him if he belongs to Marjorie and Wayne pauses for a moment, then says that, yes, he does belong to her ... in a way. So he takes her hand and tries to get her to come, and she does, just like that. And they go back down the aisle, but instead of delivering her to her mother he walks right on past, and instead of sitting back with his own family he walks past them too, beyond those standing at the back and into the lobby and out through the heavy wooden doors into the morning. Down the church steps and then onto the street. Cars lined along the road, some with their wheels on the sidewalk. She slips her hand out of his and just stands there.

There's a sun—although it's not giving off much heat—and the kind of chill that finds its way through layers, skin ... bone.

She looks at him. "I was sure it was you. Because of what I said about being a black hole and how we were better off on our own, and I thought, He's gone and done it on account of me."

He goes to speak, but she beats him to it—

"So I needed to be sure because I wasn't about Dad and then they buried him so it was too late."

Quiet for a long time. Then a butchered version of "Onward, Christian Soldiers" filters past the stained-glass windows and neither can keep from smiling.

"The funeral's sad enough," Wayne says.

Marjorie sort of laughs and so does Wayne and then they stop and stand facing each other. Marjorie says, "He had a lot of friends."

Wayne nods.

Then Kenny's just up the road and he's smoking and his sports coat is hanging open and his tie is loose and his hair's in his face. They all catch each other's eyes and, for a minute, it looks as if Kenny might take off, but then he flicks his smoke into the air and comes forward.

"Let's go," Wayne says.

"No."

"You sure?"

"Yes."

They start walking, meeting Kenny halfway. No one says anything.

Wayne looks up and sees Kenny's almost healed split lip and can't help thinking that the guy responsible is just up the street in a casket.

At last, Kenny says, "He didn't look the same."

Neither Wayne nor Marjorie speaks.

"They inject you full of shit so that you don't look anything like yourself." Kenny pauses. Brushes the hair out of his eyes and glances at Marjorie and says, "You okay?"

Marjorie stays quiet.

"I'm sorry." Then, "I've been longing to say that."

Marjorie holds Kenny's gaze. He looks away and says, "I had no idea. Swear to God." He reaches inside his sports coat for another smoke. "Stole these off my old man. He'd have a conniption."

A cloud moves in front of the sun and the morning suddenly darkens.

Kenny buttons his coat. "It's gotten colder again."

They stand there like strangers as the last tortured lines of "Onward, Christian Soldiers" are carried on the wind.

A hearse drives past and they watch it slow down and make a right into the St. Paul's parking lot.

After a long time, Kenny says, "I keep thinking how cold the water must have been."

No one speaks.

More church bells. Another hymn, and it's better, not so disjointed, the choir actually on key.

"What I don't understand is how he could keep himself under, you know. I mean ... he must have wanted to come up."

The church doors open and the priest's there. Then the casket. Carried by the wrestling team and they're wearing white gloves.

"How can he be in there?" Kenny says.

Pete's family is trailing the coffin. Behind them is the rest of the congregation, many of them clinging to shoulders and elbows and hands.

Kenny turns away and Wayne thinks he's crying, but when Kenny looks back his eyes are dry. "He was more fucked up than I thought, but he was my friend and now he's gone, so ..."

Pete's loaded into the idling hearse and the

priest waits for the mourners to gather and then raises his Bible and says a prayer and one of the wrestlers closes the back of the hearse and it pulls out of the lot and makes a left and drives past Wayne and Kenny and Marjorie, the smell of its exhaust somehow mixing with the odour of things too late to fix.

Marjorie grabs Wayne's hand. "Take me somewhere."

"Where?" says Wayne.

"Anywhere."

They start walking, leaving Kenny alone on the sidewalk.

# TWELVE

He thinks he might be holding her hand too tightly and taking the more troublesome route, but she's said nothing. Teenagers playing street hockey make obscene gestures with their sticks when they pass and, farther along, a Dutch shepherd gives chase, but its owner calls it and the dog retreats happily, its brindle tail wagging. Two ladies in headscarves tell them to get off the sidewalk if they're going to run, while an old man in a tweed cap shakes his fist in the air because Marjorie and Wayne have scared away the squirrels he was feeding.

A quick cut to the left behind the houses on Alcott Street, then across the intersection where Gower connects to Mills Crescent, past the Two Seasons Inn and the Ultramar and the Kentucky Fried Chicken with the big rock-like hole in its bucket, and past the soccer field and the hospital and the recreation centre and into the woods.

"How do you know this way?" she says, and he doesn't answer her because he has no idea how, just that he does.

Upwards now, and it's harder going, but he doesn't slow down or let go of her hand, and she's right behind him and he likes the feeling of having her close like a blanket or extra sweater. Then the trail levels out again and they run a ways farther and then emerge into a clearing. They stand there catching their breath. Then, without prompting, he's heading towards the steel ladder and he's climbing and not looking down and she's right there and it's he who helps her over this time. And they walk to the centre of the water tower and lie flat on their backs and stare up at the sky and it's a little warmer now from all the walking and climbing and the clouds have moved on, so the sun's helping.

The sounds of each other's breathing and birds and the train—loaded down with iron ore pellets— passing through. And he feels fingertips on his palm and he looks over at her and her eyes are wet but she's smiling so he shimmies closer and so does she and they're holding each other. Kissing's next and then her hand's on him and his is on her and he's not sure what he's doing only that he's doing it and she doesn't seem to be minding. And the wind whistles in their ears and she moves against his fingers and he's suddenly shivering but he's not cold and she makes a sound like there's pain but when he opens his eyes pain's not on her face.

Just lying there afterwards.

No one speaks for ages. Then at last, he says, "I thought it was you, too."

She rests her head on his chest. "You're not a black hole. I shouldn't have said that."

"It's okay."

"You're my only friend."

He looks at the sky. "You're my only friend, too."

Church bells in the distance.

Birds fly across the sun.

"Has it ever crossed your mind?"

She takes a moment, then nods. "But I wouldn't."

"Me neither."

"Big difference between thinking and *doing*."

"Yeah."

Quiet.

"Can I ask you something?" Wayne says.

"Okay."

It takes him forever, but at last he says, "Was it here? Your dad?"

Marjorie lifts her head and sits up and straightens her dress and Wayne sits up too and straightens his shirt.

They look out over Canning.

"Some sadness can't be fixed," Marjorie says.

Wayne looks across at her. Sees the man with the smile that had no happiness in it and Pete with the bad beginning and hears The Meat's second dad saying *Hug your kids tonight*. What must have gone through Pete's mind in his final moments, Wayne wonders, or perhaps nothing had.

"I picture him *alive* here," Marjorie says, "sitting like you and me. I don't understand graveyards."

After a while Wayne says, "You upset the play was cancelled?"

"A little."

"Do you think we could have won?"

"I don't know. Maybe."

"So much for St. John's."

"Yeah."

Silence.

"You would have got best actor." It dawns on Wayne then that, for the first time, he can't see the iron ore cloud and he thinks about asking Marjorie if she can, but he changes his mind because he often misses what's right in front of him.

More church bells.

A dog barks.

"I saw your mom in church," Wayne says.

"Out of her bathrobe; can you believe it?"

"She looked nice."

"They've upped her dosage. She's a little better."

He thinks of Pete The Meat and the wrestling team's white gloves and the hearse pulling away and how, in the end, Pete got a ride in a trunk of his own.

They tilt their heads back, allowing the spring sun to warm their faces.

Then Wayne pulls out an envelope.

"What's that?" she says.

"I'd intended to put it in your mailbox." He hands it to her.

She takes it.

"I've never actually given one to anybody before."

"What is it, a letter?"

He nods. "Read it later."

"I want to now."

"Later."

"Now."

"That's not how I planned it."

"What odds if I read it now or alone, they're still going to be your words, right?"

He shrugs. "I suppose."

She rips an end and blows into it and tips it over and the letter falls out and the wind almost takes it but she snatches it up just in time.

He looks away.

She unfolds it. Scans the page for ages, then hands it to Wayne and says, "You read it."

"What?"

"I'd like *you* to."

"No, I couldn't."

"Why not, Wayne Pumphrey?"

"I don't know. I'd be embarrassed, I think."

"Read, Wayne Pumphrey. I won't look at you."

"Promise."

"Yes."

"Say it."

"I promise."

He pauses. "Okay then."

Marjorie turns away.

Wayne looks down at the letter, at the handwriting that suddenly seems unfamiliar, wishing the sentences could somehow lift themselves from the page and get tossed in the wind, but then Wanda's in his ears and she's right: *No point if no one reads it.* Sometimes letters *need* to be sent, he supposes.

He breathes in and exhales and goes to start but can't, so he tries again and his voice is there and the letter goes something like this:

"Dear Marjorie,

"I'm sitting here at the kitchen table waiting to go to Pete's funeral while Wanda puts the finishing touches on Mom's hair, although I don't know why all the fuss over hair when we're off to see a coffin which has a boy inside it.

"Dad's sitting in the living room in his good suit reading that book and, although he walks around the house like his dog has died, it seems to be working because he hasn't touched a drop in ages.

"I'm not sure if you'll be there today (I'd certainly understand if you weren't) but I just wanted to say that maybe you spend too much time with Thom Yorke after all. He's an amazing songwriter, I know, but if you keep saying you're creepy and weird and asking yourself why you're here because you shouldn't be, you'll never be okay anywhere and what kind of life will that be?

"We spend so much time wishing we were somewhere else but shouldn't there be room for weirdos and creeps and anyone else, too? I mean, how many trains can we hop on and how many water towers can we climb?

"It's hard to imagine that you lived up the road from me all this time and it's only now that I'm getting to know you and I read somewhere, or maybe someone told me, that everything happens when it's supposed to—"

Wayne looks up. "You said you wouldn't watch."

Marjorie turns away. "Sorry."

"Are you mad I said that about Thom Yorke?"

She shakes her head. "Is there more?"

Wayne nods. "But I don't think I can read the rest."

"Why?"

"I don't know."

"Don't stop, Wayne Pumphrey."

He pauses. "Okay, but just to warn you, the rest came out without me thinking about it."

"*Read*, Wayne Pumphrey."

He clears his throat. "I'll take it back a bit since the last line is tied in with what comes next."

Marjorie nods.

"No looking."

She turns away.

Wayne reads:

"It's hard to imagine that you lived up the road from me all this time and it's only now that I'm getting to know you and I read somewhere, or maybe someone told me, that everything happens when it's supposed to so maybe we can't help being in each other's lives and if that's the case then it's all right by me 'cause without you I'm roast beef without gravy and tea without sugar and an ocean without a beach and I guess what I'm trying to say is: you make everything better, because before you I was alone and now I hardly ever feel that way and I wonder if it's the same with you?

"You saved me that day with Pete, Marjorie Pope, but you also saved me in another way and I hope I might have saved you, too. And Mr. Rollie was right, high school won't last forever, and soon enough we'll be grown and gone from here and doing God knows what

but I'll always remember you and I hope you will
me ..."

Wayne looks up and Marjorie's staring right at him
and there are tears in her eyes and she's smiling but
he doesn't tell her to look away.

He swallows and takes a deep breath and reads:

"I hadn't expected YOU, so it's funny how things
turn out, and I just want you to know that I'm proud to
be me and I hope you're proud to be you too, 'cause for
a couple of creeps we're doing all right.

"Your friend who thinks that, for a couple of creeps,
we're doing all right,
"Wayne Pumphrey"

# ACKNOWLEDGMENTS

My agent, Hilary McMahon, thank you for believing in and fighting for this book. Deepest appreciation to my sensitive and meticulous editor, Lynne Missen. Thank you for improving my sentences, Karen Alliston. Liza Morrison, I appreciate you making me laugh. Thank you, David Ross and everyone at Penguin, for making me feel welcome and supported.

Jonathan Watton, appreciate your reading and your honesty. My brother, Richard, thanks for the loans and the steady stream of support, and I'll pay you back, I promise. Thanks for sharing your story, Derek. And Liam Hynes, hang in buddy, okay.

And finally Michelle Latimer ... my real life Marjorie Pope.